PORTABLE CURIOSITIES

stories

JULIE KOH

UQP

First published 2016 by University of Queensland Press
PO Box 6042, St Lucia, Queensland 4067 Australia
Reprinted 2016, 2017 (twice), 2018, 2019, 2021

University of Queensland Press (UQP) acknowledges the Traditional Owners
and their custodianship of the lands on which UQP operates. We pay our
respects to their Ancestors and their descendants, who continue cultural and
spiritual connections to Country. We recognise their valuable contributions to
Australian and global society.

www.uqp.com.au
reception@uqp.com.au

Cover design and illustration by Josh Durham, Design by Committee
Author photograph by Hugh Stewart
Typeset in 11/15 pt Bembo Std Regular by Post Pre-press Group, Brisbane
Printed in Australia by McPherson's Printing Group

The epigraph to 'Two' was transcribed by the author from an interview that
Michael Cunningham gave at the Sydney Writers' Festival on 22 May 2011.

University of Queensland Press is
assisted by the Australian Government
through the Australia Council, its arts
funding and advisory body.

A catalogue record for this book is available from the National Library of
Australia.

ISBN 978 0 7022 5404 8 (pbk)
ISBN 978 0 7022 5720 9 (ePDF)
ISBN 978 0 7022 5721 6 (ePub)
ISBN 978 0 7022 5722 3 (Kindle)

University of Queensland Press uses papers that are natural, renewable and
recyclable products made from wood grown in well-managed forests and other
controlled sources. The logging and manufacturing processes conform to the
environmental regulations of the country of origin.

MIX
Paper from
responsible sources
FSC
www.fsc.org FSC® C001695

Julie Koh was born in Sydney to Chinese-Malaysian parents. She studied politics and law at the University of Sydney, then quit a career in corporate law to pursue writing. Her short stories have appeared in *The Best Australian Stories 2014* and *2015, The Sleepers Almanac, The Lifted Brow, Seizure Online, Kyoto Journal, The Fish Anthology* and Fixi Novo's *HEAT.* Julie has been a finalist in the Qantas Spirit of Youth Awards Written Word category, longlisted for the *Australian Book Review*'s Elizabeth Jolley Short Story Prize, and short-listed for the *Overland* Victoria University Short Story Prize for New and Emerging Writers. A capsule collection of her short stories, *Capital Misfits*, was published in 2015.

thefictionaljuliekoh.com

PRAISE FOR *PORTABLE CURIOSITIES*
Named a 2017 Sydney Morning Herald *Best Young Australian Novelist*
Shortlisted for the NSW Premier's Literary Awards – UTS Glenda Adams Award 2017
Shortlisted for the Readings Prize for New Australian Fiction 2016
Shortlisted for the Queensland Literary Awards – Australian Short Story Collection – Steele Rudd Award 2016
Selected for The Best Australian Stories 2016*: 'The Fat Girl in History'*
Selected for Best Australian Comedy Writing 2016*: 'Cream Reaper'*

'Darkly comedic ... combining formal inventiveness with a poker face in a particularly sharp collection of short stories.' Nicholas Jose, Best Books of 2017, *Australian Book Review*

'*Portable Curiosities* is cutting-edge writing in many ways.' Maxine Beneba Clarke, Best Books of 2016, *Guardian Australia*

'A slippery and subversive collection that made me laugh aloud as it sank a knife into contemporary Australia.' Paddy O'Reilly, Best Books of 2016, *Australian Book Review*

'Koh is a gifted satirist who makes wonderful use of language ... in this clever and highly original collection.' Kerryn Goldsworthy, *Age/Sydney Morning Herald*

'It's perfect for our busy, scary times: easily digestible and, for all its madcap imagination, utterly true.' Doug Wallen, *Guardian Australia*

'Electrifying ... a savagely brilliant exposé of society's vices.' Cassandra Atherton, *Australian Book Review*

'Armed with an uncanny ability to capture the zeitgeist ... Julie Koh's darkly satirical and convulsively funny short-story collection *Portable Curiosities* is as unsettling as it is edifying.' Sonia Nair, *Books+Publishing* ★★★★½

'Julie Koh is a rare talent. Her stories are clever, surreal and darkly funny, mind puzzles that stay with you. Koh will alter the way you see the world. There is no-one quite like her.' Amanda Lohrey

For my parents and sister,
patrons of this dark art

Contents

Sight	1
The Fantastic Breasts	19
Satirist Rising	27
Civility Place	44
Cream Reaper	69
The Three-Dimensional Yellow Man	97
Two	109
Slow Death in Cat Cafe	151
Inquiry Regarding the Recent Goings-On in the Woods	166
The Procession	176
The Sister Company	183
The Fat Girl in History	207
Acknowledgements	227

Sight

A lizard keeps following me around the house.

I tell the Tattoo Man about it when we're sitting on his verandah one afternoon. The Tattoo Man has puffy eyelids and a black beard that he strokes when in deep thought. He's in his rocking chair with a stray orange cat sitting at his feet, swishing its tail.

From where I'm sitting, I can see where the Tattoo Man starts but not where he ends. The verandah bends in the middle to accommodate his weight. If he were ever to embrace me in a bear hug, I'd disappear into the folds of his body and never be seen again.

The Tattoo Man looks like porcelain stained blue. His face is tattooed with scenes from the Yangtze River. A long boat drifts down his cheekbone, and small figures cast their fishing lines next to his right nostril. Blue dragons curl around his legs, and etched across his left arm is the face of a wrinkled, laughing man.

The Tattoo Man sets me homework.

'Watch the lizard, China Doll,' he says, looking over his wire glasses. 'Chase it into a corner. See what it does. See if it's scared of you.'

He calls me China Doll as a joke because I'm fat like he is. We both have big bellies. I laugh when he laughs, I rub my belly when he rubs his, and I yawn when he yawns. This is what we do on his verandah every afternoon when my mother thinks I am next door with Mrs Nolan eating devon and tomato sauce sandwiches.

The next day, I make my report about the lizard.

'It doesn't climb up walls,' I say. 'I chase it into corners but it won't go up to get away.'

'Good work,' says the Tattoo Man. 'That's a strange lizard.'

'I suppose so.'

'When you go home, use your special eye to look at it.'

'What special eye?' I tug on my T-shirt and turn my toes towards each other.

'Don't play dumb with me, little genius. My eye sees your eye.'

He points a finger at his forehead, and then at my belly.

At home, I find the lizard in the corner of our lounge room next to our TV.

I pull up my T-shirt and let the eye on my belly look at the lizard.

I see two things at once. My regular eyes see a lizard about the length of my forearm, its chest expanding and contracting as it breathes. But my other eye sees a little grey boy. His belly is swollen and he looks at me with saucer eyes.

I gape and he gapes.

I frown and he frowns.

I stick out my tongue and he sticks out his tongue.

He looks like a normal kid but I can't see any feet on him. His legs seem to fade away as they get closer to the floor.

I report to the Tattoo Man the next afternoon.

'As I suspected,' he says, folding up his newspaper. 'A bad case of black magic.'

★

Third eyes run in the family, on my mother's side.

They're usually located somewhere on the forehead but not in our family.

My third eye sits on my belly, where a belly button should be. It enjoys rolling around. I like this eye more than my other two. It winks at everyone in the room, even if it doesn't get any winks in return.

My older sister used to have an extra eye peeping from her left shoulder.

Her third eye had a combative gaze. It glared at people. It made her shrug her shoulder all the time, involuntarily. It was high maintenance.

The first time my mother realised something was not quite right with my sister was when she picked her up after her first day at primary school. My sister said she had spent the afternoon playing with new friends. They were amazing, she said. They could take their heads off and bounce them on the ground like basketballs.

There were other signs. My sister never wanted to be dropped off at the mangroves bordering the far side of the school, and she never used the school toilets.

My aunts reassured my mother that she would grow out of it — that a third eye dims as one gets older, and will only regain its sight when one is weak and old, dying in hospital, unable to push the devils away from one's bed.

My sister asked for her shoulder to be fixed. She wanted to be like the other girls. She wanted to explore the mangroves with them without being teased. She wanted to lick the salt from the tree leaves without seeing women perched on the branches above her, holding their severed heads out as gifts.

When she came home from the operation, I said: 'How does it feel?'

'How does what feel?'

'Your eye?'

'They're fine,' she said, rubbing the two on either side of her nose.

I wondered where they put the eye after they cut it out.

I wanted to ask her where it was, but her remaining eyes had a glassy film over them. She had passed into the world of the normal, where I couldn't reach her.

*

When my grandmother was alive, I liked watching TV with her in our lounge room.

One night, a beautiful black-haired lady came by, her white gown flowing. The bells on her wrists and ankles rang in my ears. The air around us smelled like jasmine.

The beautiful lady touched my grandmother's forehead. My grandmother didn't notice.

I rushed up to the lady and tried to kiss her cheek before she vanished. But I was too late.

My mother was standing in the doorway, and saw my lips touch the blank air.

'It was a beautiful lady with bells,' I said. 'I've never seen anyone so perfect.'

'A person who can see goddesses can also see devils,' said my mother. 'That third eye is a curse. We will have to close it or put it out.'

I didn't know what she meant by putting it out. It sounded like she wanted to leave it on the doorstep like a cat, cold and shivering. My third eye started to water.

'You keep that eye covered, do you hear?' said my mother. 'It isn't a thing that nice people talk about. It isn't decent, especially on a fat belly like that. You keep it to yourself.'

'Did you ever have a special eye?' I asked.

'Mine was on my chest, near my heart,' she said. 'It saw devils paint the walls of our house with the blood of the family cat. It saw car crashes the day before they happened. It saw the ghosts of women who'd been burnt to death in house fires. Nice little girls shouldn't be exposed to these things.'

'But they happen, don't they?'

'If this is the world, I don't want you to see it.'

★

Another reason my mother doesn't like third eyes is that she doesn't like excess. She likes order, cleanliness and special rules.

She gets rid of all the loose change in her purse, and she cuts all the fat off pork chops. Her hair, our furniture and our garden hedges are all arranged at right angles.

She is always in the midst of what she calls an eternal battle against flab. Every spare minute she is doing a sit-up. I count them with her.

She says it's better than yoga. Yoga is too slow. Yoga doesn't burn fat fast enough. Yoga, according to my mother, needs to be done at six times its prescribed speed, more in the style of karate.

My father's explanation for my mother is that she's highly strung. He says there is an old Italian master hovering on the ceiling of our house, on call to restring my mother when necessary, as if she were an expensive violin.

My mother always says she married my father because he had no balls.

I believe her. She wouldn't want balls in the house.

She hates games.

*

A dead man and woman and girl moved into our house a year ago.

They looked more or less regular except I couldn't see their feet and they had a habit of walking up walls. At the beginning of their stay, I used to turn my head to the side to imagine what it might be like living sideways.

The ghosts like rapping their knuckles against the

underside of the floorboards, and leaving their breath on the bathroom mirrors.

Sometimes the appliances in our house go on the blink. The toaster will spit bread prematurely, or the gas stove will ignite whenever a plane flies over. When these things happen, I wonder if the other family is bored, or having a bad day.

I don't think the ghosts are related to each other but I like to think of them as a family.

I didn't talk to my mother about the ghosts. She hated hearing about my third eye and had started referring to it as my 'imagination'.

I didn't want to distract her anyway. She was about to have another baby. Her belly was swollen and ready to pop. I liked patting it and feeling the baby move inside.

My mother was sitting on the couch one day when I turned on the TV. A Japanese warrior was surrounded by enemies. He had his sword unsheathed and the veins on his neck bulged.

'Turn that off,' said my mother. 'No violence while I'm pregnant.'

I obeyed.

'Why?' I asked.

'A mother needs to be calm during pregnancy. She has to look at flowers and beautiful things. A baby born to a woman who sees ugliness will be ugly. A woman who gazes on a face that is covered in moles will have a baby covered in moles. What you see is what you get.'

'If you look at ghosts, will your baby be a ghost?'

'I want you to be a nice, good girl,' said my mother. 'No more crazy talk.'

'What's wrong with questions?'

'The way you are is unnatural,' she said, resting her palms on her belly. 'I blame myself. I collected flowers from frangipani trees while you were in the womb. The fragrance got into your brain and twisted it.'

Our house had a spare room.

One morning, the week the baby was due, my father put on overalls and brought in a ladder, masking tape, newspaper and tins of paint.

As the sun set, he embraced my mother in that room, the walls newly blue.

He left a white cot in the corner and hung a parrot mobile above it. He filled a small chest of drawers with disposable nappies.

Stencilled white aeroplanes flew along the four walls, and a laughing clown popped out of a clock near the window to mark each hour.

The new baby never arrived.

What arrived instead was a pale version of my mother.

She had gone to hospital suddenly, and came back grey.

She lay in bed and I held her hand.

'Was it that bad movie we saw?' I said. 'Is that why the baby didn't come home?'

She closed her eyes, her hand limp in mine. My father

picked me up by my armpits and set me down elsewhere.

'Watch some TV,' he said.

Soon, my mother felt ready to shower with me again.

She put on my shower cap, pink with blue daisies, letting the elastic snap into place on my hairline. Standing in the shower, our backs against the spray, my mother scrubbed me like we were under a steaming waterfall and I was her mud-caked village ox.

She didn't tell me to close my eyes to keep out the shampoo, like she used to. She didn't speak at all.

I spent the time looking down at the tiles and wondering why my mother had bruises all over her shins.

Blood swirled in the water splattering around my feet.

I didn't ask any questions.

We were clean and we were silent.

★

The Tattoo Man is telling me about black magic.

'A man who practises black magic can cast a spell that causes a pregnant woman to miscarry,' he says. 'The soul of the child then becomes his property.'

The Tattoo Man rolls a cigarette, lights it and offers it to me. I inhale and cough.

'In this way, a man can assemble a household of half-borns, who take on the appearance of lizards. Under his control, they are forced to creep into the houses of others and steal. If they fail to return, he finds them and cuts their throats. When there is no money left to extract from the neighbourhood, he gathers his lizards and moves on.'

The Tattoo Man holds out his hand, and I give him the cigarette.

'Only those with special eyes can see these children. Go back and make friends with the half-born. Your house has trapped him.'

My mother is hanging out washing when I come home from my visit.

'You weren't at Mrs Nolan's,' says my mother, straightening out a skirt on the line. Her voice is thin and quiet. 'In fact, she says you haven't been visiting her for weeks. You've been going somewhere else every afternoon.'

'I've been talking to the Tattoo Man.'

'Who?'

'The one down the road.'

'That crazy Chinaman with the blue face who shouts at people on the street?'

'He's not crazy.'

'What have you been doing there?'

'Talking about magic.'

She takes me by the shoulders and shakes me. 'Has he fiddled with you?'

'No!'

'Stay away from him. Mrs Nolan says he's just out of a mental home. I won't have a daughter of mine running wild around this neighbourhood. I don't want the neighbours thinking all Asians are the same.'

She lets go of me and picks up a dropped peg from the grass.

'Magic,' she mutters, shaking her head. 'Your imagination

is getting away from you. You better catch it before I do. Because if I get my hands on it, I will strangle it.'

★

The lizard boy doesn't frighten me, even with those big saucer eyes.

He just follows me around the house like he always does.

I teach him things sometimes. I show him the video game I'm playing on our TV, where I'm a plumber dressed in red and white and I go around hitting my head against bricks and jumping on mushrooms.

'You could have been the green plumber,' I tell him.

'Who are you talking to?' asks my sister.

At bedtime every night, I carry the lizard boy to the cot in the blue room where no one goes anymore.

I tuck him in and tell him everything's going to be all right.

★

My mother is shouting.

My father stands in the blue room with her, saying: 'It's just a lizard.'

'Don't hurt him,' I plead from the doorway.

'Is this another special friend?' says my mother.

I shrug.

'Well, it's not welcome in this house, do you hear?' says my mother. 'Men with tattoos! Ladies with bells! Lizards in cots!'

One hand is on her hip and the other against her forehead.

'It's not your fault about the baby,' I say. 'It was black magic.'

My father looks at me. 'Take this lizard out.'

I pick up my friend and leave. I stand outside the room and watch my parents.

My father is trying to hug my mother.

'I'm fine,' she says. 'Don't touch me.'

She pushes her wrists hard against his chest and says nothing more.

★

My mother's bruises are getting worse.

The lizard boy is the cause of it. He clutches her legs as she does the housework. She wipes down the kitchen sink, sweeps the floor and dusts the curtain rails, and all the while he digs deeper into the skin around her ankles.

'What bruises?' she says when I point them out. 'I don't see any bruises.'

'Yeah, what bruises?' echoes my sister.

I introduce the lizard boy to the other ghosts in the house.

He can't walk up walls with them but they wave to him and smile from their sideways world.

Yet despite his new family, he still won't let go of my mother.

My family is sitting around the dinner table, eating.

'I saw a dress I want,' says my sister.

'Toilet paper is getting too expensive,' says my mother.

'The price of water is going up,' says my father.

'I don't want to do any homework,' says my sister.

'It's time to prune the mango tree,' says my mother.

'The apples I bought are going soft,' says my father, 'why isn't anyone eating them?'

In the same room are the ghosts, sitting at a table on the wall.

They copy everything my family says.

The girl talks of dresses and homework. The woman talks of toilet paper and pruning. The man talks of water and bad apples.

The woman is adamant about cutting that mango tree down to size, as if she really can do it.

'There's another family in the house,' I say. 'They're sitting on the wall having dinner.'

My family slices its steamed fish and crunches its broccoli and says nothing.

The lizard boy crouches under the table, clutching my mother's ankle.

I save part of my dinner and leave it on the floor of my bedroom for the boy.

I don't know how else to help him.

My mother discovers me doing this. 'What's going on here?'

'It's for a cat.'

'How does it get into your bedroom?'

'I leave my window open.'

'Whose cat is it?'

'Dunno.'

'Is it really a cat or is it another imaginary friend?'

'Yes, it's a cat. It's orange. And I don't have any friends.'

My mother folds her arms. 'I haven't seen a cat around.'

'Here, it scratched the windowsill.' I point to needle marks I once made when I was bored with backstitch.

'Don't feed cats or they'll keep coming back.'

'But it's starving.'

'That cat is someone else's problem,' says my mother. 'If you help one, the hordes will come.'

'What about cats that don't belong to anyone?'

'That's their bad luck,' says my mother.

The lizard boy lets go of my mother's legs.

He crouches in the cupboard under the stairs and won't come out.

I watch him in the half-dark, and he watches me. He flickers. I see him as an older boy, a teenager, a young man and as an old man.

Then he goes back to looking like a little boy.

'I see what you mean,' I say. 'You would have been handsome and strong.'

★

I wake in the night with pains in my belly that make me double over and cry out. My third eye squints and smarts. My forehead is hot.

'I'm taking you to the hospital,' says my mother.

'I'm not going,' I say.

I scream for my friend but he doesn't come.

The emergency doctor speaks with my mother and nods.

I am wheeled into an operating room and the anaesthetic kicks in.

When I open my eyes, the surgeon is making an incision in my belly. Out of it she pulls my third eye.

'You've been a bad girl,' says the surgeon. She tosses my eye to an assistant, who laughs and tosses it to another.

'Catch!' shrieks the assistant, but the other misses.

I can't see where my eye lands.

I wake again and am looking at the ceiling.

I can't move. Tears are rolling down my face. I can't lift my hand to wipe them away.

A nurse notices I'm conscious and says: 'Oh, my love.'

She wipes one side of my face and then the other.

'Everything's okay, chicken. No need to panic. You'll be able to move again soon.'

My mother is at my bedside. 'You're a brave little girl,' she says, running her fingers through my fringe. 'It was for the best.'

I don't believe her.

Some cord has been cut, and whatever has been taken is now alone somewhere in the darkness.

My parents stop on the way home to pick up chicken broth that neighbours have made for me.

'It'll make you stronger,' says my mother, through the car window. 'I'll only be a second.'

I hear her talking to the neighbours about an appendix.

As I wait, an old man covered in tattoos shouts at me from his verandah.

'My eye sees your eye.' He points to his forehead and then to me.

I turn away, groggy.

When I look back, he has vanished.

I don't know about any eye.

I will become a girl who sits at the kitchen table every night and talks about dresses.

An orange cat is sitting on our front doorstep, next to a white cot. It swishes its tail at me.

'Whose cot is that?' I ask, bundled in my father's arms.

'Someone's coming to take it off our hands,' he says.

A lizard the length of my forearm is lying at the feet of the cat, decapitated. Ants are swarming over the body.

'Cats kill lizards?' I ask.

'They do it to please, I think,' says my father. 'I'm sorry about your lizard.'

'My lizard?'

'We have a surprise for you,' he says. 'You're getting to be such a big girl we decided it's time you have a new room.'

My father carries me down the hallway to a cold space painted blue.

The window of the room looks out onto the front doorstep.

I watch my father sit there with his head in his hands until a car pulls up. A young man gets out, hands my father a twenty-dollar note and carries the cot away.

My father's shoulders shake.

I pretend not to see.

★

In the shower, my mother is being careful not to scrub too hard.

'I don't want to hurt you,' she says.

I am silent.

I listen to the spray of the water against our bodies and the hum of the exhaust fan above our heads.

The next shower I insist on having alone.

'Don't touch me,' I say to her, when she goes to put on my shower cap.

I am the one to snap the elastic in place, and I am the one to put my mud-caked back against the waterfall, and I am the one to walk past the laundry acting like I can't hear the muffled sobs of my mother coming from behind the door.

★

In the blue room, I dream of a porcelain man. His face is covered with scenes from the Yangtze River.

'This world is two worlds,' he says, 'and the divide between them is finer than a layer of human skin.'

'Here we are laughing,' says the man, pointing at the face of a laughing man etched on his arm. 'And here we are crying.'

He takes a penknife and cuts a slow, deep line through the face of the laughing man. Blood spills out, a thick red stream.

He passes a hand over the laughing man, and the stream vanishes.

'Something is wrong with those who won't see the laughing, and something is wrong with those who won't see the crying. Don't play dumb with me, China Doll.'

He lifts me by the armpits and puts me on his workbench.

He takes out his gun of shuddering ink, and brings the tip to my skin.

I struggle but he holds me firm.

A blue eye forms on my belly.

The Fantastic Breasts

So I see this pair of Fantastic Breasts one day.

I'm at a conference, in the foyer, pinning on my name tag. A hundred plain-looking, spotty breasts are milling about, sipping chamomile tea from styrofoam cups. They're all wearing far-sighted spectacles that magnify their nipples. The topic of the next session is The Difficulties of an Objectified Existence in a Patriarchal World, whatever that means. Everyone's standing around commiserating and consciousness-raising, which is getting them so heated their spectacles are fogging up.

I down my espresso and think about the whole sorry affair. What's sorry about it is that I'm really scraping the bottom of the barrel at this conference. I've taken a big risk in going where few men have dared venture and it's turned out to be a disappointment: the probability of finding a bit of good-quality breast here among the styrofoam is negligible. I should have known better. After all, I've had a lifetime's experience passing from chest to ample chest, in pursuit of that one perfect set of breasts to have and to hold. But, for some reason, A-grade breasts have continued to elude my grasp. I begin to wonder if

I should unpin my name tag and abandon the noble quest forever.

Then, all of a sudden, I spot these Fantastic Breasts, so fantastic they deserve a capital F and a capital B. They come tottering out of nowhere on gazelle legs, backed by a caboose that fell from a peach tree in heaven. The Breasts bound and quiver in slow motion like no others can. They are full cream milk.

They're so swollen it's like the Global Breast Incubator pumped them with excess milk, let them ripen a little longer than usual, scooped them off the great conveyor belt, screwed them onto that pair of stilt legs and gave them a slap on the rump to get them going on their merry way.

I'm hooked. Staring into that cleavage, I see my voluptuous future. There haven't been breasts this fantastic since the beginning of time.

The Fantastic Breasts are all-rounders, a supernaturally talented two-for-one deal. They don't have a voice but, boy, can they tap dance! Between them, they can pick a matchstick off the ground. They've won three Olympic golds on the uneven bars. They can mime from memory the value of π to a million decimal places, two decimal places at a time. They can play Beatles records with their nipples without wearing out the grooves.

Though located in Sydney, the Fantastic Breasts can launch themselves high enough to get a bird's-eye view of Tokyo. Sometimes they drop in on a Giants baseball game at Tokyo Dome and catch a fly ball at the wall while standing at home plate.

The Fantastic Breasts are such knockouts they're a mythology in themselves. There's even a comic book series based on them.

In the first frame, a guy is kicking a vending machine in a dark alley. It's out of order. The guy's Coke is stuck.

A shadow looms behind him.

HANDS UP. TURN AROUND. DON'T TRY ANYTHING CLEVER.

The guy does as he's told.

The shadow comes into full view, wearing a grotesque dolphin mask and pointing a gun right at the guy's guts.

GOLLY, says the guy, quaking in his boots. *IT'S THE DOLPHIN!*

A drop of sweat rolls down the side of his face.

Suddenly – POW! SLAM! BANG! The Dolphin's cheek is on the bitumen, pinned there by the stiletto heel of a studded, black patent leather, thigh-high boot.

This boot belongs to the Fantastic Breasts.

Fluorescent light from the vending machine illuminates the Fantastic Breasts for titillation. Stunning in their symmetry, they spill out over their skimpy (yet surprisingly supportive) bulletproof bra, which is dominated by black latex and diamond spikes.

Snow falls from the narrow sky above the alley. The Breasts haven't even bothered putting on a trench coat. They're kept hot by the steam rising from their own skin.

HOW CAN I THANK YOU, FANTASTIC BREASTS? asks the guy.

The Fantastic Breasts kick the vending machine. Cans rattle out. The guy gulps. The Breasts hand him a Coke and take a few more for the road.

Then, in one bound, the Fantastic Breasts are gone.

Hollywood adapts the comics into the blockbuster hits *The Fantastic Breasts*, *2 Breasts 2 Fantastic*, *The Fantastic Breasts 3: Tokyo Drift* and *The Fantastic Breasts: Redid, Redone & Rewound*.

They also make *The Fantastic Breasts: First Dawn*, which takes us back a generation to where the feud with the Dolphin all started on the dusty plains of somewhere far, far away. The film reveals that the Fantastic Breasts and the Dolphin were childhood playmates and friendly chess rivals before a catastrophic event defined their allegiances and changed their destinies forever.

As the films progress, the Fantastic Breasts perform increasingly mind-boggling feats in slow motion, saving the metropolis one arousing quiver at a time.

In the final scene of *The Fantastic Breasts: Redid, Redone & Rewound*, one breast wraps itself around the mainmast of a ship like a boa constrictor, functioning as an anchor for the other breast to stretch a kilometre and pluck a drowning child from the middle of the Indian Ocean. The Fantastic Breasts, in an amazing revelation, also turn out to be inflatable and motorised, guiding the distressed ship to safety despite the best efforts of the Dolphin and his seafaring cronies to sink the vessel.

The closing credits roll. The theme song kicks in: half sax, half sex.

In the bonus DVD feature, *The Making of the Fantastic Breasts*, the producers discuss how they screen-tested every A-list set of Hollywood breasts for the role but discovered none fantastic enough to cast.

The producers recount to the camera how they pled with the Fantastic Breasts to play themselves in the title role. The producers look at each other knowingly, cross their arms and grin. They tell us they got their way in the end, and that casting the Fantastic Breasts as the Fantastic Breasts turned out to be a masterful stroke of filmmaking – a giant leap forward for twenty-first-century cinema.

The producers fail to mention, however, the TV spin-off series they financed, which stars a less fantastic set of breasts and which has found itself playing 3 a.m. TV slots a little earlier than anticipated.

Although the Fantastic Breasts save the world by day, they're mine by night.

I serenade them under the stars in the middle of a Roman piazza. I dine with them in a candlelit garden, where a lute player perches on the side of a fountain and strums Renaissance melodies. I feed them strawberries and chocolate truffles on Saturday nights. I whisper them sweet nothings. I grow them English roses and carpet the bedroom with petals. I present them with my great-grandmother's rings. I praise their kindness, generosity and intelligence; let them precede me into lifts, through doorways and railway ticket gates; converse with their less well-endowed friends at interminable dinner parties; cuddle them when they're not in the mood; and listen to their rants about the inconsiderate citizens of the metropolis.

Every evening, without fail, the Fantastic Breasts and I go out together for a stroll. People marvel at their charm and at how proud I must feel to be the companion of the Fantastic Breasts. At home, we sit by the fire and I tell the Fantastic Breasts how beautiful they are. The Breasts curl up against me like helpless, blind puppies.

But sometimes, when I'm feeling down, I start thinking that the Fantastic Breasts aren't all that fantastic. I begin to think they're getting full of themselves and I wonder who they think they are, going around assuming they deserve a capital F and a capital B and thinking they can parade me around the streets like some sort of trophy.

So I take them out for a walk and when people start gawking I whisper sweet nothings to the breasts like Stay, Sit, Fetch, Heel, Roll Over and Beg.

And when I tire of that, I put them back in the bedroom and say Lie Down and I whisper that they dress like they're asking for it and that they're looking flabbier these days and that the producers called earlier to ask why they're so out of shape and I whisper to the breasts that I saw them flirting with that extra on set I'm not stupid I see what's going on and maybe it's my fault for assuming I could expect more from breasts that make the lewd sort of movies they make and then I start feeling a bit better about myself and even a bit like a superhero and I push the breasts up against the wall and hold them there and they squirm and their boots can't touch the floor. Then I release them and the breasts start getting their clothes together and stuffing them into a big bag and I punch a wall and I shout where are you going you don't have any real friends and all your money's in my bank account and I punch another wall to match the hole in the first one because of course I like symmetry and then the breasts cower against the wardrobe and so I stop punching holes and sit on the bed and sob into my hands and promise I won't do it again and I say I know it's my problem I'm messed up and will they forgive me I'm only being protective because I love them too much and I can't help it I'm jealous of any man who even looks their way and I never meant to hurt them and I only want what's best for them and please remember the serenade in the piazza and the English roses and my great-grandmother's rings and the strawberries and the chocolates and all those times I sat through interminable dinner parties with their friends and how if you add all that time and effort up it shows I love the breasts more than any other breasts in the universe.

And when the breasts have stopped trying to self-harm by throwing themselves against the wardrobe and the windows and the bathroom mirror and when I've got them down on the carpet and they're a bit calmer, I remind them they're not babies anymore, they can't be so emotional, they're embarrassing themselves by being such drama queens, all I wanted was to conduct a normal conversation like normal grownups do, that I only start these conversations sometimes when I'm feeling down, that a guy needs to be able to vent his feelings once in a while without the threat of breasts going psycho, that it's not like I even beat them up, and I also remind them of how much I care about them even though they're so sheltered from reality they don't even realise no other man alive would treat a pair of breasts like them so well, and they should always remember there are other breasts out there who'd be grateful to have a man as loving and protective and understanding as I am.

Then I forgive them for making such a disgraceful scene and I cuddle them and let them lie against me again like helpless, blind puppies.

And as I sit there, stroking them to sleep, I think about how the Fantastic Breasts need me and how the metropolis, in turn, needs the Fantastic Breasts and therefore how, without my continued commitment to the care of the Fantastic Breasts, the metropolis faces doom. Then I close my eyes and I don't feel so bad anymore, comforted by the knowledge that I am the manliest manly man the world has ever seen.

But a man who is the manliest of manly men must also think responsibly about the future of the metropolis. So I start considering how in-built obsolescence is a fact of life and how mammary glands are no exception to the rule. And I decide that, once the Fantastic Breasts begin to slouch and sag, and when they begin to miss the fly balls at Tokyo Dome, and when no one marvels at them anymore when I take them out for a stroll, I'll need to begin keeping an eye out for a more youthful, more fantastic set of breasts that are likely to come tottering out of nowhere, preferably a set synthetically enhanced so that they depreciate in value at a much slower rate than the ugly old hag of a set I once picked up at that miserable conference on The Difficulties of an Objectified Existence in a Patriarchal World.

Satirist Rising

She has a strange feeling about the man sitting next to her on the skyglide.

He is dressed in a three-piece tweed suit and a red bow tie. His grey hair is slicked back.

He is eating a courtesy packet of peanuts and thumbing through an old copy of *The Self-Fulfilling Prophecy*.

From the corner of her eye, she watches him rub his thumb against his fingertips to rid himself of the salt. Under the overhead reading light, the cufflink on his left sleeve gleams at her: it is the head of an onyx panther baring ivory fangs.

He stands in the next line at Immigration. He inches forward with her until they are both at the head of their queues.

She waits for a family of four to move through the gate. Then it is her turn.

She wheels herself forward.

'Evie Bluhm?' says the machine.

'Yes.'

'Enjoy your stay in Auckland.'

At the baggage carousel, he waits next to her.

He steps forward and pulls a tan leather suitcase off the moving belt.

Instead of hurrying off, he lingers. He doesn't look at her but stares at other people, at the ceiling, at the same bags going around and around.

She squints at the carousel and sees her own luggage approaching.

'That's it,' she says, pointing it out to the airport ambassador who has been assigned to help her.

Hers is a frayed plaid polyethylene bag, half-full. The ambassador hooks it over the back of her wheelchair.

'Wow,' he says, 'you're smaller than your own bag.'

'Thanks.'

'Have you ever thought of getting a spaceframe? Wheelchairs are seriously old-school.'

'If you've got the cash for one I'd be delighted to accept it.'

The ambassador laughs. He wheels her out of the airport and onto a shuttle, where he secures her wheelchair and wishes her a pleasant stay.

As he hops off, the man in the tweed suit hops on. He tosses his suitcase onto one of the luggage racks and sits down opposite her. He pulls a spiral notepad from a pocket inside his jacket and jots something down.

He doesn't acknowledge her presence, but the other passengers stare. A young boy tugs on his mother's sleeve and points. Those gammy legs, those tumours pushing out of her neck, those strange little bumps multiplying under her skin, those bulging, asymmetrical eyes. A festival of deformities, all gathered on one little old lady.

The shuttle reaches the centre of town. The access ramp extends onto the kerb for her.

The man in the tweed suit alights at the same stop and follows her up Mayoral Drive.

He is still following her as she wheels herself through the front doors of the hotel.

He queues up behind her at the reception desk.

She glances around the foyer. The hotel looks stuck in the past – clean but in need of a dramatic update.

'Good morning, Ms Bluhm,' says the concierge. 'Welcome to Curiosity Inn.'

'Thank you.'

'I noticed you've been admiring our foyer. As the world's most avant-garde boutique hotel chain, we at Curiosity Inn pride ourselves on our cutting-edge retro design concepts. For each of our sites this year, we've re-created the atmosphere of a typical four-star hotel circa 2015.'

'Why four-star not ...'

'Sorry, ma'am?'

'Never mind.'

'Would you like a complimentary newspaper, Ms Bluhm?' The concierge gestures to a stack of folded broadsheets on the counter. 'We're pleased to publish the news in the format of that era.'

She glances at the front-page headlines: 'US Government Ice Cartel Launches IPO'; 'Lesser Flamingo Crowned New Prince of Spain'.

A third article gracing the front page features a shot of the recently elected Australian Prime Minister. He is lying naked with a come-hither smile, a national flag artfully covering his private parts. He is on a bed of flags, on a floor of flags. The caption says he is ready to confide in his beloved compatriots the economic benefits of climate catastrophe. The headline of the article is 'I Love a Sunburnt Country'.

'Ms Bluhm? A newspaper?'

'I think not,' she says.

The concierge takes her bag and reassures her it will follow her up to her room shortly. He hands her a plastic card in a small cardboard folder.

'Here's your swipe card,' he says. 'You're in a Wheelchair Accessible Room with City View. It's on the eighth floor. Room 870. Enjoy your stay.'

She wheels herself towards the lift. As she leaves, the man in the tweed suit walks up to the counter.

'Good morning, sir,' says the concierge. 'Room 846 is available for you today.'

She watches the number above the lift decrease from 11 to 10 to 9. The number hangs. She eyes the strange tweed man.

He is still at the counter with his back to her, sorting through some papers.

Her hotel room is very 2015. There is something consoling about it. A regular double bed with crisp white sheets, a bolster and two rows of pillows. A desk with a Curiosity Inn writing pad and a cheap plastic pen. A bar fridge filled with

Coca-Cola and soda water, and assorted snacks including a cylinder of stackable potato chips.

The window's fauxview is set so the room looks out over a historically accurate city street and, in the distance, a motorway. Above the motorway are green road signs bearing white arrows and the names of unfamiliar – perhaps now obsolete – roads.

In the bathroom is a GROHE hand shower, a hairdryer and a variety of toiletries in small bottles and boxes. One of the boxes is labelled *Shoe Sponge*. She isn't sure what to do with it. She wants it to say *Shower Cap*. She hasn't brought one.

She undresses. In front of the mirror, she unwinds her bandages. She peels the sheet of green gel protectant off her chest and stares at the spreading, gaping sore under it, which refuses to heal. She replaces the gel sheet with a new one.

'It's a good day,' she tells herself. She tries to smile then notices a new tumour forming on her neck, expanding by the second. 'It's not a good day.'

She transfers herself from the wheelchair to the seat under the shower.

The water falls. She sits still, staring at her body in the bathroom mirror.

Later, she watches TV, tuning in to the local accent. She reapplies her bandages while watching a DIY lifestyle segment on building a statement outdoor table setting. Another channel is screening a movie in which a woman sets fire to the curtains of a hotel room.

She lies on the bed and picks up the telephone. She holds

the handset to her ear, listens to its low purr, puts it down and falls asleep.

When she wakes from her nap, the room is warm. She doesn't want to leave.

She wipes on some foundation. It sinks into the creases of her face, covering none of her imperfections.

It will have to do.

A staff member from the hotel stands at the entrance to the conference function room, next to a silver A4 poster stand. The sign is printed with the words: *The End Game Leadership Series.*

'Ma'am,' says the usher, eyeing the tumour trying to push its way out of her neck. 'Are you lost? The Curiosities are upstairs.'

'I'm here for the End Game session. I'm the talent.'

'Oh, I do apologise, I assumed ...'

'What are these Curiosities?'

The usher points to a poster on the wall.

The Portable Curiosities, it says. *A Public Warning.*

'It's a travelling exhibition, sponsored by the United Nations and run in partnership with Curiosity Inn. It berths at all our hotels around the world. It's free to the public, if you have time.'

'I suspect I do.'

'They're currently installed on the tenth floor in the East Gallery.'

There is introductory text at the gallery entrance but she wheels past it.

A series of large black boxes is arranged in rows across the floor.

On the front panel of each box is a small viewing window.

She peers into the first.

Under a spotlight, an elderly man in a nappy sits on a rotating golden disc. His skin is a sickly white, his muscles wasted. He is miming with great concentration. With both hands, he seems to be twirling an invisible stick on its axis, keeping it horizontal at all times.

In the second box is an old Asian lady. Her long hair, parted down the middle, hangs like two white curtains over her nappy. She sits wide-eyed on her rotating disc, watching her right hand move slowly through the air, twisting and turning, fingers separating and coming together. It is as if she has never seen a hand before.

In the third box, a black man with a white beard, his nappy discarded on the floor, has stepped off his circular platform and is pacing his box. Side to side, forward and back. His hands are clasped behind him and he speaks continuously, although she can't hear anything he's saying. He pauses occasionally to shake a finger at an imaginary audience.

She knocks on his window but he doesn't notice her.

'I predicted you,' she says.

She knocks harder.

'I predicted you,' she repeats, raising her voice.

He continues to pace and talk to his audience.

'It looks like a mental asylum,' she says to herself.

'Crazy old mimes, eh?' The usher from downstairs has

suddenly appeared next to her. 'Your session is about to start.'

★

There are just three people in the audience.

She watches them from the stage.

Two sit next to each other in the front row. They wave at the interviewer and blow kisses.

The third is the tweed man. He is sitting in an aisle seat in the last row, flicking through his notepad.

'Welcome to this session of End Game,' says the interviewer, crossing her legs. 'Today we have as a guest a woman who needs no introduction. The most notorious satirist in the world, once described as mankind's most dangerous individual, appears as a guest of Curiosity Inn – Where Curiosity Will Get the Best of You.'

'What a slogan,' says the satirist.

'You're ninety-seven years old this year,' continues the interviewer. 'Let's rewind almost a century and revisit your childhood in Tasmania. Any early memories?'

'When I was born,' says the satirist, 'the doctor held me up to the light and said that it was unfortunate. I was Libran, he told my mother, with Satirist rising.'

'You mean Sagittarius.'

'No.'

The interviewer shifts in her seat and scans her notes. She clicks a button on a small remote, and an image appears on a large screen behind her.

'This is a photo of you as a child,' she says. 'A very pretty girl.'

'I was extremely vain.'

'You look quite different these days.'

'I grow uglier by the second.'

'How is that possible?'

'My work is a special kind of demon. When I point out ugliness, I, too, grow ugly. When I cripple with my words, I, too, become lame.'

'What do your friends say when you come to dinner with a new deformity?'

'Dinner? Friends?' The satirist snorts. 'Nobody stays friends with a lady devil.'

'It can't be that bad. There must be people who haven't abandoned you.'

'I keep myself clean of responsibilities to individuals. I've shed friends in order to protect them.'

The interviewer raises an eyebrow. She clicks the remote again. The next image appears on the screen. It is the cover of a book – black with the title in bold, white capitals.

'This is, by far, your most famous work,' says the interviewer. '*The Self-Fulfilled Prophet*, first published in 2015.'

'You mean *The Self-Fulfilling Prophecy*.'

'Sure. Talk us through the origins of the book.'

'Where to begin?' The satirist leans back in her wheelchair, crosses her arms. 'The *Prophecy* was a satirical future history. It purported to be based on the movement of the planets. It was structured as a day-by-day, month-by-month and year-by-year account of the future, arranged by star sign. But as the world lost its imagination, the book was reinterpreted as actual prophecy. People began to remake the world in the image of the book. They started nonsensical wars that I'd plucked out of my arse. The Six-Point Pan-Amphibian Crusades. The Smaller Greater Peninsularis Conflict. History repeated itself in progressively absurd iterations. News headlines were copied straight from my work.'

'It's rather a sweeping claim, isn't it? That the world might have religiously copied your fiction?'

'Have you even read the thing?'

'So you're saying the landscape of your satire has been mapped out before your very eyes.'

'Worse still, the world has gone beyond the *Prophecy*, to a point of no return. It's a headless beast that keeps on charging. I'm to blame for a future I sought to prevent.'

'Speaking of guilt,' says the interviewer, 'you've been on wanted lists all over the world. Tell us about that.'

'In the early years, assassins hoarded copies of the book. Those who lost the wars wanted to lynch me. They saw my pen as a bloodied sword, not the scalpel of a surgeon.'

'How then were you able to travel here?'

'I've been in hiding for many years. But when there's a need to travel, I do so under false identities. The instability of my appearance is helpful in this respect.'

'How have you felt about your exile from Australia, in particular?'

The satirist shrugs.

'How does anyone feel in exile from their homeland? One never fully adjusts. One always yearns, forever adrift. I laugh at my country from afar so that I don't have to weep for it.'

'If you could go back, would you?'

'Revisiting could be a mistake. I suspect that all that remains of the place is an intellectual black hole. Besides, as I grow older, I wonder if my exile isn't merely geographical. When I think about it, I've been in exile my entire life. Always on the fringe, never at the centre.'

'Given the suffering that appears to be inherent in your line of work, why did you choose to fulfil that initial prediction at birth that you would become a satirist?'

'I wouldn't say it was a choice.'

'Well then, when did you realise you were one?'

The satirist falls silent. She looks out towards the back of the function room, searching the past.

'You know what?' she says, finally. 'The moment one stops crying and begins to laugh that hard, dark laugh is the moment a satirist is truly born. For some it takes an intimate betrayal, an unjust death, even a full-blown war. It's always the idealist who falls furthest from the state of grace, the one whose pen turns from a long-stemmed rose into a polished blade.'

The interviewer sighs. 'And on that positive note,' she says, 'let me open the floor to questions.'

The tweed man gets up from his seat.

He strides over to a microphone in the aisle.

He smiles.

'Your prophecy states that satire will end,' he says. 'That the last satirist, wanted by many, will surrender, marking the end of true civilisation. Do you consider yourself to be the last satirist?'

'I would hope not.' The satirist's cackle, low and hoarse, cuts through the room. 'Although it's quite possible that

I no longer have a function in this society. That in a society beyond satire, my existence is entirely irrelevant. It's possible I'm no longer considered such a threat.'

'To whom will the last satirist surrender?' asks the interviewer. 'The secret police?'

'It's a puzzle yet to be solved. But if I were indeed the last satirist, and if an end really were approaching, wouldn't it be curious if, out of the blue, after all these years in the wilderness, I received an anonymous invitation to a series called End Game, a private farce designed as a ruse to lure me out of hiding. Wouldn't it be fascinating if someone with a unique sense of humour decided to arrange one last interview for me, to be given unwittingly to an audience of actors. Someone who enjoys elaborate schemes has brought me here. Someone who wants to tease me with the prospect of one last captive audience, who desperately needs to indulge in the thrill of the chase, to watch me wriggle in the trap. A hunter raising his rifle. A clear shot ringing through the air.'

'Why might one accept such an invitation? Could this be interpreted as surrender?'

'A satirist never surrenders: she only makes practical decisions. Perhaps she wanted to stay in a nice hotel room, to order an all-day breakfast from room service one last time. She might have been seeking the perfect ending to her own story, and the opportunity might have presented itself in an envelope bearing the seal of Curiosity Inn. After all, the life of a satirist must be as tragic as her satire, don't you agree? Her end must be a perfect joke.'

★

'Ma'am, room service.'

She reties her robe and opens the door. A young man in uniform stands in front of her, carrying a tray.

'Courtesy of the gentleman in Room 846.'

He walks briskly over to the table by the window, and sets the tray down.

'Is there anything else I can do for you, ma'am?'

'That's all, thank you.'

She watches him leave.

She lifts the silver cover. Underneath is a white plate loaded with bacon, poached eggs, mini sausages, hash browns and toast, all topped with a sprig of parsley.

A note is tucked under the plate. In immaculate copper-plate handwriting, it says:

A last supper and last prediction.
You will come of your own free will.

She pulls open the paper flaps on a packet of butter, takes a knife and begins to spread the butter over the toast. She cuts everything on the plate into small pieces, watching the yolks spill out of the eggs. She begins to eat. She crunches on a bit of bacon, chews on a bit of sausage.

She lays the note out in front of the plate and eats, reading and rereading it. She works through everything on the plate, leaving the hash browns until last.

Stomach full, she sits back and watches the sun set over the motorway.

She leaves her tray out for collection. The young man

is waiting cross-legged on the hallway carpet, reading the *Prophecy*.

★

A fire alarm rattles in her ears.

She squints at the bedside clock. Past midnight.

She finds her robe and swipe card, and wheels herself out of the room.

It seems everyone on the floor has left before her. The lifts are out of the question. She opens the door to the fire escape and peers in.

A boisterous line of Curiosities is making its way down the stairs. Still in their white nappies, they throw their arms over each other and laugh. A woman is scatting. Another backflips down the steps. A man with a moustache and creaky limbs dances the flamenco, clicking his fingers and tapping his feet as he descends.

There is nothing she can do but wait and watch.

One of the Curiosities, the man with the sickly white skin and wasted muscles, stops to consider the satirist and her wheelchair.

'I'm of no use,' she says. 'There's no reason to save me.'

'Why would you assume I want to save you?' he says.

'Right.'

He shakes his head and giggles. 'I've never met anyone so fatalistic.'

He pulls her onto his back and adjusts to her weight. He plods down the stairs, one landing after another.

'You were in the exhibition,' she says. 'Who are you?'

'I'm the last glass artist in the world.'

After a few flights, he stops, wheezing, and sets her down.

'I can't go on,' he says. 'We'll have to leave you here to die.'

'Fine.'

He giggles again. 'I've never met anyone so gullible.'

A stout woman ambles down and hoists the satirist up over one shoulder as if it's no big deal.

'This is the last potter,' says the glass artist.

The potter continues down the steps like clockwork, turning abruptly at the end of each flight.

At the bottom of the stairs, they push through the final exit onto the street. The Curiosities gather in groups, chatting and ignoring the cold. There are more of them than she thought: perhaps fifty or so. One has brought the satirist's wheelchair, and helps her into it. They all introduce themselves and shake her hand – everyone except the Asian lady, who stands apart, staring into the distance.

'That's the last performance artist,' says the potter. 'She's exploring internal energy this year, so she has a policy in place of no bodily contact. We think she might actually be crazy.'

The last historian – the one with the white beard – asks the satirist if she is the author of *The Self-Fulfilling Prophecy*. 'We heard she's visiting. But it's hard to know what she currently looks like.'

'Never heard of her, or the book,' she says.

'It's only the greatest satire ever written,' says the glass artist. 'Through it, I peered into a new universe.'

'It's true,' says the last abstract painter. 'The satirist rises and the rest of us follow.'

The concierge emerges from the hotel. He apologises for the false alarm and announces it is safe for guests and exhibits to return.

The Curiosities turn towards the open door of the hotel.

'Where are you going?' asks the satirist. 'Can't you escape?'

'We're stateless,' says the glass artist. 'We're possessions, not people.'

'Surely you can hide.'

The historian shrugs.

'We're perfectly content in our cells. There aren't any locks. We're no longer dangers to society, just a collective warning about wayward irrelevance. No one bothers us. We're fed and clothed. In the back panels of our boxes, we each have a mat for sleeping, a hose for washing, and a hole for shitting. In exchange for participating in our own public ridicule, we can practise our respective disciplines.'

The satirist frowns. 'A terrible compromise.'

'One doesn't always receive the type of freedom one expects,' says the glass artist. 'The *Prophecy* I spoke of predicted our freak show, but what it didn't foresee was that the landscapes of our minds would continue to flourish. Mighty glass oceans, darting glass clownfish, swaying glass sea anemones. A glass ship that sails forever towards the horizon. My prison is my patron.'

★

The satirist applies another gel sheet to the wound on her chest.

She winds fresh bandages around her torso.

She moves out of the bathroom and over to her bag. She feels around for her best dress and puts it on.

She picks up the phone.

'Room 846, please.'

'Yes, ma'am. Please hold the line.'

He answers.

She clears her throat.

'You are the last collector.'

'I am.'

'And I am the last satirist.'

'You are. The final piece in the set.'

'Well, then,' she says. 'Come and collect me.'

She looks into the mirror and chuckles at the thought of a satirist who no longer rises but only rotates – a pig on a vertical spit.

Her laughter rings out, high-pitched and clear, like that of a small child.

Civility Place

Breakfast is last night's leftovers.

You leave your plate in the sink and splash water over it. You brush your teeth. You rub gel between your palms, work it through your hair, and use a comb to arrange a neat side part. You cut Friday's dry-cleaning tags off your suit. You straighten your tie. You pick up your bag, sling it over your shoulder and walk to the train station.

Thirty seconds after you arrive on the platform and walk to the point where you know the first door of the first carriage will open, the train arrives.

You're on your way to work.

The entrance to the tower comprises six revolving glass doors. Their action reminds you of hand-cranked egg beaters, or one of those spy films where the hero is stuck in a tunnel in his battered suit, pitted against wind and gravity and tonnes of water that are bearing down on him and forcing him closer and closer to a giant fan with rotating blades.

You can feel the egg-beater fans sucking you in.

Whump, whump, whump.

You look up for a second at the tower looming above you. It's so tall that you can't see where it stops and the sky begins.

You steel yourself and walk in, preparing to be served as suggested – beaten or chopped.

On the front desk in the foyer stands, as usual, an extravagant floral arrangement. Today it's an immense concoction of birds of paradise.

'Welcome to Civility Place,' grins the concierge, who is standing to one side of the flowers.

'Hi, Serge.'

As usual, you stop to ask after his motorcycle.

He once showed it off to you at the end of his shift. As it gleamed in the artificial light of the car park, he told you how he often took it on holidays up the coast to a little shack that looked out over the ocean, and how he was planning to ride it overseas one day – maybe around Japan.

Serge smiles when you enquire after the bike's health. He says it is well. He is, however, thinking of selling the bike. He wants one that's just a bit shinier and louder. The head of the tower's security team has hinted to him that a promotion might be on the cards if Serge continues to demonstrate outstanding commitment to his role. A promotion would give him some extra cash for a new machine.

'Wow, that's great,' you say.

'Thanks, I reckon it's almost in the bag,' says Serge. He nods to others passing by. 'Welcome to Civility Place,' he says, giving them the friendly grin of recognition you had thought was reserved for you alone.

The lift greets you good morning in a recorded female voice, smooth and mature.

Beth from Banking steps in and greets you too. She has a voice similar to the recorded female voice. You wonder if she could simultaneously be a lawyer in your building and the smooth-voiced woman trapped in the walls of the lift.

You are close enough to Beth from Banking to be able to smell her shampoo and whatever expensive scent she has on. As you inhale, you look at her pearl earrings and down at the spikes of her patent black heels, which have those red undersides you noticed once in a training seminar when she crossed her legs and arranged her impossibly straight chestnut hair.

Beth from Banking is a woman made for this building.

The glass of this place is in her DNA.

The lift zooms into the sky.

They say these lifts are the fastest in the country. They're not as fast as they used to be, though. Rumour has it that they had to be slowed down because some chump couldn't cope with the speed and threw up all over the lift buttons.

The entire building, including the lifts, is made of glass. The internal walls are glass, the conference tables are glass, and the desks, doors and shelves are glass.

Even the floors and ceilings are made of glass, and there is an unspoken but unpoliced rule that one must never look up the skirts of the women on the floors above.

You've been told that a middle-aged woman was once found wedged in one of the glass ceilings, her legs hanging down into the lower floor, still in motion as if walking, and the top half of her engrossed in flicking through a file. She licked the tip of her index finger intermittently as she read, unaware of the consternation surrounding her. No one knew how she got there, and the resulting rescue services bill was enormous.

As you are taken up to Level 403, you see the surrounding city. All roads lead to this tower, and all the buildings look as if they were forced to part to accommodate this monolith as it erupted from the ground.

The lift announces your level and you step out. As levels go, it's not a very prestigious one. Your team has a reputation for bringing in less money than others, hence its relegation to this floor, where a view of the outside world is only possible when the whole level isn't engulfed by clouds.

They say that on Level 1200, at the very top of Civility Place, one is able to dictate letters to clients while looking across into the infinite blue and down onto rolling carpets of clouds as if one is God. No one you've spoken to has ever been to Level 1200 but they all suggest that to arrive at that point in your career, you would have to have parted ways with your soul.

You walk through the automatic sliding doors and past the kitchen. Two secretaries are discussing hypo-allergenic varieties of lip balm while hovering over the daily fruit box. You excuse yourself, reaching between them to take a banana.

This would never happen on the higher levels. You don't know what it's like on Level 1200, but you've heard that on Level 1199 the secretaries never utter a word. They don't even arch their eyebrows so as not to cause any disturbances to the flow of the rarefied air.

The day at work begins like any other. Perhaps the air conditioning has been set one or two degrees colder than usual, but otherwise everything is normal.

You settle into your death chair. You call it this because – although it's handsome and designer – it will eventually kill you: first by weakening your spine and then by rolling its five vengeful chrome wheels in starfish formation over your vital organs.

You start up your computer and open your inbox.

A query from a prospective client awaits you, as well as thirteen replies from existing clients concerning urgent matters. There's a joke email about metaphorical flying hippos, forwarded to you by a friend you've been trying to shake. Another chain email appears, courtesy of your aunt, which describes the wonders of a Mayan superfood that can make your hair sprout faster in all the right places and reduce your risk of oesophageal cancer by 43.8 per cent.

You open the firm's time and billing software.

You've already wasted one six-minute unit of billable time imagining a giant hippo falling from the sky onto your unwanted friend, and another two units wondering how the Mayan superfood is able to distinguish between right and wrong places for aggressive hair growth.

You record these three units of time to Office Administration and forward the prospective client's email to your secretary, Mona, asking for a conflict check.

You want to focus like you usually do but somehow you can't. You stare at your computer screen and nothing registers. The words begin to float and rearrange themselves.

Through the multiple glass walls that separate you from the outer offices, you watch two window cleaners hanging in harnesses on the outside of the building, drawing squeegees across the windows. They can't see you – the tower's exterior is all mirrors. It's so high up that they're breathing oxygen from tanks on their backs. The wind is strong and the cleaners swing like pendulums, sometimes smacking right into the building with loud thuds. No one in the outer offices seems to notice them.

Mona knocks on your door, handing you a file you need.

'Shocking working conditions,' you mutter. 'Shouldn't they be on some sort of scaffold?'

'What?' she says, then follows your line of sight to the window cleaners. 'Oh, they'll be right – they're foreigners. They probably come from some place with super-huge mountains. Plus, where they're from, they're probably used to getting smacked around.'

'That's outrageous,' you say.

You don't like Mona. She's only been working for you for a couple of weeks. She's the replacement for your old secretary, who accidentally suffocated last month in a room full of files. The firm has since toyed with the idea of transitioning to a paperless office, partly to prevent further losses of human resources.

'It's not outrageous,' says Mona, crossing her arms. 'You're just being politico correct, or whatever.'

You turn back to your computer screen and hear one of the cleaners crash again into the glass.

'I tell you what's outrageous,' Mona adds. 'It takes them a whole year to clean this building.'

You've heard this before – that once the window cleaners get to the top, they begin again at the bottom, after being allowed to break for two hours on Christmas Day to carve a turkey and wear ill-fitting paper crowns liberated from shiny red-and-green crackers.

One of the emails in your inbox is an urgent follow-up query from a client who is a national distributor of fruit juices.

You don't care about the juice company. Its CEO is upset that another juice company is using a logo of an ugly orange cow with bad teeth, which he believes is deceptively similar to his company's logo of an ugly purple cow with bad teeth.

The slogan at the bottom of his sign-off is: *Everything you could have asked for, and more.*

You don't understand how this slogan can be true in any respect. It's not even real juice this company sells. It's cordial, basically, with a barely qualifying squeeze of third-rate fruit.

You open a new email window.

Dear Mr Laing, you type. *Your cow needs a dentist.*

You stare at the screen and yawn so much that tears run down your cheeks. You hold down the delete key until the window is blank.

You call Haline's extension.

'Coffee?'

'See you in the foyer. Give me five.'

You watch the time in the corner of your computer screen. One minute. Two. Three. Four.

You grab your jacket and walk to the lifts.

Today at the cafe underneath the tower, the barista is the bearded one with the eyebrow ring. The quality of this guy's coffee depends on his mood, and he's looking grumpy this morning.

Haline looks over her shoulder to check who's in the line.

'Everywhere I go in the city,' she says to you in a low voice, 'I see this fucking tower. I can't escape it.'

'Well, it *is* twelve hundred storeys high.'

'With a frigging spike on top of that.'

'You could just not look at the skyline.'

Haline squints. 'You know,' she says, 'I closed the curtains last night to get away from it. Then I turned on the TV and it was in the opening credits of that shit spin-off, you know, where that cartoon pen draws the skyline? It took a whole four seconds to finish the spike. I could've thrown the TV through the window and jumped out after it.'

'You're not going to jump out any window,' you say. 'Right?'

'I've worked it out,' says Haline, handing exact change to the girl behind the counter. 'If you factor in the extraordinary amounts of time we spend at this place, we're being paid six dollars an hour and we're being charged out at three hundred. By the collective sweat of our junior white collars, we are paying for Phillips Tom's boathouse and his third wife's fake boobs and his sons' private school educations and his extended family's annual A-reserve opera subscriptions.'

'So what are you going to do about it?'

'God knows. It could be too late to leave. Plus I don't know if I have it in me. They hire masochists like us for a reason.'

'I don't think I could find another job,' you say, taking your flat white and nodding to the scowling barista. 'The longer I do this, the more specialised I become. So far, all that my professional skill set amounts to is an unparalleled knack for spotting similarities between pictures of cows.'

'Speaking of jumping out windows,' Haline murmurs, 'remember Windy?'

'Who could forget Windy,' you say.

With coffees in hand, you and Haline wait for a lift. When one arrives, you both make way for a gaggle of winter clerks who strut out, on their own caffeine run. These are the top law students in the city, and over these few weeks between semesters the firm is showing them the incredible lifestyle that they, too, could have if they decide to accept a job at Civility Place pending completion of their degrees.

'Smug little shits,' says Haline, as the doors close. 'Did you hear one of their induction modules is Aerial Yoga for Stress Management? One day they'll realise no one here gives a flying fuck about people who can only function properly in Suspended Updog.'

In the Level 403 kitchen, you take a sip of your coffee and realise the milk in it is burnt. You pull the plastic lid off the cup and pour what remains down the sink.

'I can't bear to start work,' says Haline. 'Let's go see Pravin.'

You drop into Pravin's office and ask about his weekend. 'What weekend?' he says. 'I haven't left since Friday.'

'That's terrible,' says Haline.

'It's okay,' Pravin shrugs. 'I'm getting efficient. Now I spend every waking minute doing work, and I've done an online course on lucid dreaming that's shown me how I can hang out with mates while I'm asleep. So I still have a sort of social life. Wild times, actually, all while taking naps under this desk. Boy, did I dream we got smashed last night.'

Your attention drifts. You stare at the collage on the wall of Pravin's office.

It's part of the firm's billion-dollar art collection, which has been built with the dual aim of Supporting Artists while Creating a Vibrant Office Environment. The initiative not only enhances the mental health of the firm's employees but also satisfies the artistic yearnings of those with an imaginative bent, allowing them to integrate creativity into their working lives without having to sacrifice income or material comfort.

The collage in this office appears to depict a giant black Scottish terrier standing in an empty courtroom contemplating a strung-up Mussolini. It's an artwork that Haline has nicknamed 'The Scottie Dog of Fascist Depression', which she declares is the work of an obscure dead artist,

Sad Hamish, who was probably told as a child that he was good with scissors when, in fact, he was not, resulting in a misguided commitment to collage as a literal means of cutting-edge artistic and political expression.

Back at your desk, you attempt, unsuccessfully, to angle your computer screen so that it faces away from passing colleagues, and you spend two unbillable units of time reading articles online.

Floods, the Middle East, an Australian exclusive on Michael Caine. There is a picture of the actor from the late 1960s in which he is surrounded by women wearing tight, white high-waisted pants with the word *ALFIE* emblazoned on their left buttocks.

You snap out of your reading spree when you get to a tragically boring opinion piece on modern Benthamite prison architecture.

Overcome with guilt at wasting more time, you close the window on your screen and look out the glass door, watching all the people pretending not to be watching you.

You hope a warning hasn't flashed up on the screen of anyone downstairs in IT, alerting them to your extra-curricular reading.

Every hour, on the hour, you go to the toilet, just to take a break.

On your third visit today, a senior partner strides in and unzips his fly at the urinal next to you.

It's Phillips Tom. He's never spoken to you before, even though you are in his practice group.

'Morning,' he says.

'Morning.'

'Lovely day.'

'Yes it is.'

'Chin Lin Rao, isn't it?'

'Ah, it's Rao Lin Chin.'

'Lin, how are you enjoying your career?'

'It's going very well, thanks … Phillips.'

'Good. Good to hear. Bright young fellow like your-self – you could be moving up in this little tower of ours in no time. You know, Lin, I should get you involved on a new matter for Xynorab. We'll be working with their lawyers in Beijing. How are you placed for a conference call at seven on Wednesday morning? Do you have capacity?'

'I have a few things to—'

'It'll be a valuable learning experience. You should be on the call.'

'Ah, then,' you say, 'I have capacity.'

'Good. That is very good to hear.'

Two streams drum against the glass urinals and drip to a pause.

By the time two o'clock rolls around, you have finally begun reworking your first billable piece of correspondence for the day.

Dear Mr Laing, you type.

A profound start.

But you're starting to feel strange. Your chest feels tight.

You take your hand off the mouse and put both palms flat on the table to steady yourself. You feel as if you might start hyperventilating and indeed you would, if you weren't surrounded by colleagues. It's becoming apparent to you that you may be having a mild panic attack.

You don't understand why this is happening. You've spent years at this desk feeling completely fine and this has hardly been a stressful day in comparison to all the others.

You glance at the other lawyers perched on their death chairs behind their glass doors, tapping away at their keyboards. No one else seems panicked.

This is, after all, Civility Place.

You go to the kitchen to make some chamomile tea. Maybe that will calm you down.

Your hands tremble as you take a cup and plate from the shelf and pull a tea bag from its individual paper envelope.

As you fill the cup from the tap, you wonder why the tea isn't turning yellow and then realise that you have your thumb on the button for cold water.

Just your luck – the firm's Managing Partner also seems to have had an urge to make a cup of tea, and is approaching the sink where you're standing.

You've never seen him on this floor, nor up so close. Usually you watch him from afar giving an official welcome, or see him in videos that screen on loop in the kitchen, delivering firm-wide news updates for staff.

You turn to the Managing Partner and force a smile, while your hands, cup and plate shake and clatter.

He considers you, clearly unaware of who you are.

'Nice to run into you again,' he says. 'How's your career going?'

'It's going very well, thanks, John.'

'Great,' he nods. 'Brilliant.'

Your hands are still fumbling around. You spill the tea, which lands all over John's designer shoes and socks. Panicked, you grab a paper towel and zone in. But John is there before you, of course. He is, after all, a Partner and a Managing one at that.

'I'm so sorry,' you say, as he cleans himself up.

'Lucky your tea's cold.'

John looks at the paper towel in your hand and you realise that you've forgotten to tear the towel from the dispenser and that the entire length of the roll has extended towards his feet.

'Having one of those days?' he asks as you both straighten up.

'I've certainly had better.'

You grin through the panic. You're bursting out of your skin. You want to run right out through the automatic doors to the nearest lift. But you stay standing there, trying to sip the cold tea but finding it hard to connect with the teacup.

'Must be motion sickness,' you explain. 'From the building? Shaking in the wind ...'

'Yes, a wonderful innovation, isn't it?' says John, taking over at the sink and making himself an Earl Grey. 'A flexible building. Who knew anyone would be able to design a swaying tower that can withstand even earthquakes. Too bad for you, eh?' John claps a firm hand on your shoulder and guides you over to the window, through which you can see parts of the city.

Your body feels scattered and numb, almost like it's shutting down.

'This firm has strong roots,' says John. 'Just like this building. We have unmatched staying power, even in adverse conditions.'

He sticks his hands in his pockets and draws his shoulders back, standing tall. 'Look out at this city. Look at how we rise so powerfully above the rest. How do we do it? Through an unshakeable commitment to the provision of top-quality services for our clients! Long after we're both gone, this firm will still be expanding of its own accord, its cogs turning, fuelled by the sheer talent and dedication of hardworking, intelligent people just like yourself.' He puts his hand on your shoulder again. 'Now, why don't you call it a day? You seem like you need a good half-day off.'

'I don't think I could do that. I have deadlines.'

'You know we're serious about mental health, don't you? We're big on that work–life balance thing. We take pride in caring for each other at this firm.'

'Yes.'

'So I think you should go home.'

'I can't leave my work to other people.'

'You can log on remotely, can't you? That way you can meet your deadlines *and* get some rest.'

'I suppose so. I suppose I should go home.'

'Good idea,' he smiles. 'Go get a life, then. Go on, you.'

★

You return to your office.

You pick up your keys and drop them into your back pocket. You do the same with your mobile. Then a blue pen. Then a black pen.

You start grabbing every item within reach and filling your pockets with them. Highlighters, Post-it notes, even a red self-inking 'DRAFT' stamp. Anything and everything goes.

Why are you panicking? You still don't know.

The glass around you hums – your panic is vibrating through the building. It stretches all the way down into the roots of the tower and further.

Your panic is bottomless and so, it seems, are your pockets.

The more items you drop into them, the more room your pockets seem to have. Postage stamps, paperclips, pencils, free two-packs of Anzac biscuits from the kitchen, the banana from the fruit box, your landline phone, a heavy-duty hole puncher, your in-tray, manila folders, binders from your shelves, an old, annotated *Corporations Act*. Your chair even fits into the right outer pocket of your jacket without touching the edges. You slide your computer screen into one of the inner pockets with no problems at all.

The more you panic, the less people notice you. Not even the secretaries sitting right outside your door turn their heads. *Clickety, clickety, click*, go their computer keys. Lawyers are returning to the floor through the automatic doors, holding their coffees out in front of them and failing to see you pick up your desk, turn it on its side, and lower it, legs first, into your pants. You are sweating. The air conditioning is raising goose bumps on your skin.

You keep at it until you've cleared everything.

The entire office is now in your pockets but your pockets look like they're completely empty.

You still haven't calmed down. You gulp down the rest of the cold tea – it dribbles down your chin – and you slide open your office door. You walk neatly and urgently out of the office, through the automatic doors, to the lifts, through the egg beaters and all the way down the hill to the station.

On the train, the carriage is almost empty.

You rest your head against the window.

A man has followed you in. He's wearing a brown parachute tracksuit with fluoro green stripes. The pants have been cut off above the knee, probably with an axe.

He sits right next to you, despite the spare seats. He breathes down your neck. He smells like cigarettes and beer and last week's fried chicken. He stares at you and rubs his crotch.

You are suffocating. You pull open a carriage window and the air that blows in is warm and also smells of nicotine and alcohol and oil.

You hold your hands in front of you. They're still trembling.

You burst out of the train three stops early and walk, dizzy, through the afternoon all the way to your front door, tracing the railway line to keep your sense of direction.

For some time, you sit on the couch in your living room, staring at the curtain.

Eventually, your deadlines come to mind. You reach into your back pocket for your remote access token. You need it to access the firm's intranet from your home computer.

Instead, your pocket produces a set of pencils, Post-it notes, the red 'DRAFT' stamp, and an ergonomic keyboard made in the shape of a wave.

'Fuck.'

Next the computer screen comes out, followed by a glass filing cabinet.

It takes the whole night to empty your pockets. Your remote access token is nowhere to be found.

The complete contents of your office are now in your living room.

'My God,' you say, when you check your pockets one last time and pull out the heel of a shoe, followed by the secretary attached to it.

Mona straightens up, pulls down her skirt and smooths her hair. 'Here's that conflict check. I only just got around to it. Oh, and your remote access thingy.' She hands you the token and some crumpled printouts, then walks off to the kitchen.

'How did ...' you say. 'What are ...'

You touch the back of your hand to your forehead. It feels both hot and cold. If you were to average this out, you think, you might have a temperature of no medical concern.

You change into your usual striped pyjamas, wrap a blanket around your shoulders and pull the death chair up to your computer. You begin the email to the purple cow juice company once again.

Dear Mr Laing, you type. *We refer to your email of 31 July.*

A purple cow is chewing on grass and begins nibbling on your fingers but its bite isn't clean, it's crooked, and you are so appalled by the jagged mess those teeth are making that you wake yourself up to find that you've been drooling on your keyboard.

You wipe your cheek with your forearm and hold your hands up to eye level against the morning light. You try to will them steady but they continue to tremble. At least your fingers are still there, and the nightmare cow isn't.

Phillips Tom walks by, zipping up his fly and wrinkling his nose at your striped attire.

'Settled in for the night, did we?' he says, and exits via the bathroom door. 'I have a new matter for you, by the way,' he calls out from the toilet. 'Tell me you have capacity.'

Hot on his trail is a highly strung Scottish terrier barking out numbers in Italian from one to six, its tail wagging from side to side in time with each bark.

You feel weak but you can't afford to take any more sick leave.

You don't bother with breakfast. You change, comb your hair, straighten your tie, pick up your bag and leave the house.

Halfway down the street, you have a strange urge to look back at your apartment block.

It shimmers, mirror-like, and seems to be expanding upwards.

You turn and hurry to the station, telling yourself that it's a hallucination, that it will be better when you return, that some screw – probably made of glass – has come irretrievably loose inside your head.

The lift in Civility Place declares that it is a good morning and makes a favourable comment about the weather.

'Morning,' you reply.

'Your target for today,' says the lift, 'is 26.4 billable hours, taking into account yesterday's unmet target.'

To your surprise, your office is just as it usually is.

Everything you put in your pockets yesterday is back where it used to be. Your computer is plugged in. The stationery spread out on your desk quivers, itching to be used.

As you contemplate the scene, you try to slide your hands into your jacket pockets but your fingertips can't seem to find the openings.

In fact, all of your pockets have closed up – sewn shut like those of a new suit.

You sit at your desk thinking about Windy.

Windy used to be a Senior Associate at the firm. Her name was really Wendy but she was from New Zealand.

Windy wasn't like Beth from Banking. She was dumpy, eccentric and an oversharer, and more often than not sported ladders in the calves of her stockings.

Windy complained daily of feeling sick in her stomach.

'I just can't work out what it is,' she said one day, leaning over her secretary's desk. She clutched her belly, which had swollen to the size of a gigantic inflatable beach ball but hadn't yet developed multicoloured stripes.

'Women hold stress in their stomachs,' declared her secretary.

'It can't be stress,' said Windy. 'It's probably indigestion.'

'Every day of the year?' you asked. 'Maybe it *is* stress.'

'It has to be indigestion,' said Windy. 'I can't afford to be stressed. I have a mortgage to pay.'

She pulled out her purse, twisted the clasp and flipped it open, revealing a crumpled photo stuffed into a plastic insert.

'This is my house,' she said.

'You keep a photo of your house in your purse?'

'It motivates me to come to work.'

She handed you her purse and you took a closer look at the picture.

'Hang on, this isn't a house. It's Civility Place.'

'What?' She grabbed it back and stared at the photo. 'You're right. How strange. When I first moved in, it was a cottage.'

The secretary rolled her eyes. You watched her open a new window on her computer screen. *Psycho*, she typed and clicked *send*.

Another secretary halfway across the floor laughed out loud.

'So,' you joked, 'every day you've been catching trains from work to work from work.'

'I suppose so,' said Windy. 'I've never noticed. I'm so tired these days. I don't look up at the sky anymore. Are there any stars left?'

A week later, Windy was in the middle of asking her secretary to order her a monitor-riser when she stopped abruptly.

Then she let out a shriek and proceeded to run silently in rectangular patterns around the edges of Level 403, slamming into the intervening glass, over and over again, until paramedics arrived.

It was impossible not to see and hear Windy's meltdown through the walls, floors and ceilings. Everyone pretended she was simply not there. They sidestepped her as they went about their important filing and practice group meetings and two-unit coffee runs.

That night, the cleaners sprayed each of the affected glass walls and windows, and wiped them down with chamois cloths. They removed the cheek marks, the nose and chin marks, and the palm marks with the splayed fingers.

'At least we know it's suicide proof,' said Phillips Tom.

All day you think of the cleaners removing Windy's marks from the glass.

At five o'clock you pick up your keys and wallet. You leave your jacket on the back of your chair, a trick one of the guys once taught you, which apparently suggests to passers-by that one is still in the building when one is really out doing other things, like having a hotel quickie with the new girl from Payroll.

You wait for a lift. Phillips Tom is already there, jamming his thumb against the up arrow.

He looks at you with narrowed eyes and then, with a disdainful flourish, checks the time on his watch.

'I,' you mumble, 'I have a medical appointment.'

'We have that conference call with the Chinese at seven tomorrow morning.'

'I'll be on time.'

'Good,' says Phillips Tom. 'Now, go get a life.'

Serge is standing in the foyer, as always, with his hands resting in front of him, one over the other. You take him aside.

'I need your bike.'

'Pardon?'

'I need it right now,' you say. 'I can pay you half of what's in my bank account. You can buy twenty bikes with it.'

He picks up a phone concealed behind the birds of paradise.

'Rob?' he says. 'Can you cover for me?'

You've been passing your wallet from one hand to the other, and Serge notices they're trembling.

'You okay?'

'I have to get out of here.'

'Follow me,' he says.

In the car park, he asks where you're going.

'Far away. All those places you talked about. Tokyo, maybe.'

You transfer him the money on the spot.

'Have a good trip,' winks Serge, handing you a pair of aviators. 'Send me a postcard.'

Aviators on, you are riding out of the city, past beaches and over mountain ranges, and the whole time you are singing 'Serge, Serge, the concierge', and you are overtaking slow trucks on highways, and you are passing bright lights and small towns, and the sun is warming your back, and the wind billows inside your shirt, and the air is crisp, and the birds are calling.

You are taking trains and buses and boats, and you are crossing seas to places where people offer you food in strange tongues and write you directions in unfamiliar scripts, and your hands are steady, and your soul is lifting, and the smiling face of a once young pop star with white teeth and white wings appears against a fluffy white backdrop of clouds and sings gently to you about a summer holiday in a place where the sun shines brightly and the sea is blue.

And then you slow down and begin to walk, and you discover a billboard filled with white-panted women, and you spy the word *HOTEL* emblazoned in bold on their buttocks, and the billboard is pointing you to an arched hedge.

You wander down the green tunnel and it is rustling around you, and you are dreaming of white high-waisted pants and white terry-towelling robes and white bubble baths and crisp white sheets when you begin to hear a familiar *whump, whump, whump.*

There, at the end of the tunnel, are those six revolving blades.

Serge is standing in the foyer, one hand resting over the other. The birds of paradise seem to have been rearranged by an ikebana artist of unsound mind. Their stems have been driven into metal stakes and they peck at each other as if in pain.

You find you are wearing a sleek new suit and holding an expensive briefcase in one hand.

'*Konnichiwa*,' says Serge, bowing. 'Welcome to Civility Place.'

You say nothing in response. You take off his aviators, drop them on the glass floor and crush them with the heel of your designer shoe.

'Shame,' says Serge. 'They weren't a bad pair.'

A stream of Beths from Banking, wearing shiny black heels with red undersides, clack past you to the lifts. You follow them.

'Good morning,' says the lift in its smooth voice. 'Phillips Tom is waiting for you in the conference room on Level 1200.'

Around you, the Beths assemble. They take sips through straws from bottles of juice branded with ugly purple cows with bad teeth.

'What flavour is that?' you ask them.

'Fruits of the Valley,' they say.

'Does it really taste like fruits from a valley?' you ask. 'What fruits even grow in valleys?'

'It's everything we could have asked for,' they say in the voice of the lift, 'and more.'

As the doors close, the automated voice of civilisation announces that you are rising to Level 1200, to the very top of the hill, to the very peak of the world, into the clouds, into the sky, and beyond.

Cream Reaper

I've spent just five minutes in the presence of the man known as Bartholomew G, and I'm already convinced he's a special kind of genius.

The famous allure of this titan ice-creamer is hard to deny. Forget the Romans: this suave thirty-four-year-old is the new man of modern empire, the greatest food revolutionary of his generation, a self-described food futurist slash visionary educationist who has Sydney in the grip of a deluxe ice-cream pandemic. So far, his empire stands at five Ice Dealerships, whipping up frenzies in Alexandria, Surry Hills, Bondi, Darlinghurst and The Star.

The man with the finger on the pulse of frozen desserts has cleared his usually frantic schedule to give me this exclusive on a pop-up venture he is trialling this week. He's granting me no-holds-barred access to follow him and his team over the venture's first five days. He's already calling me his 'embedded journalist'.

I can barely contain my excitement. Not only is this my biggest assignment yet but I've also dabbled in a bit of horrifically bad homemade ice-cream in my time. I could do with some professional tips.

We're standing in front of the security gates of G's new digs in Alexandria, waiting for his business partner, Ian Lee, to arrive. When I comment on G's individual style, he launches into a rundown of his outfit for today – a dark green Acne Studios fine-knit merino wool sweater over a white A.P.C. shirt, ASOS slim dusty-pink chinos rolled at the ankle, and a pair of Tod's tan suede moccasins. He's rocking Cutler and Gross tortoiseshell glasses and a pompadour cut so sleek he reckons it gives David Beckham a run for his money.

'You know,' he confides, 'true style is a core life skill. It's all about mixing high- and low-end brands. Plus if you can add a compelling op-shop find to your ensemble, you're more than ready to step out the door.'

I tell G that I'm in awe of the empire he has under his belt, which is continuing to expand with no signs of flagging. I ask what drives him to succeed.

'I came from nothing,' G shrugs. 'All I'll say is that Dad cleaned shopping centre toilets. But I've always thought ahead of the curve. Years ago I had this epiphany. In the near future, we weren't going to have newspapers with food lift-outs. We were going to have foodpapers with news lift-outs. Who wanted to read about the Middle East anymore? Food was where it was at.'

It turns out G is a polymath of sorts. With a degree in pharmacology, he began his career in pharmaceutical research before making a dramatic switch to pharma-degustation, apprenticing at Louis Vian's two-Michelin-star London restaurant, Opioid, in the late 2000s, then getting runs on the board at fine-dining establishments Kurohiko,

Grästerika and The Merry Axolotl. He credits Opioid with instilling in him a deep respect for each ingredient, honed while working under the watchful eye of Vian, who insisted that each dish be served in a blister pack of ten softgel capsules.

G's luck changed in 2013 after a near-miss scooter accident grazed his leg. He quit as sous-chef at The Merry Axolotl and returned to Sydney to get back to basics: artisanal ice-cream, his one true love. It also eventually meant uniting with his pal Lee for today's joint venture.

'Speaking of the Dude Food Devil,' says G, as Lee finally fronts up.

Lee is a member of the hot celebrity set G runs with – known among foodies as The Golden Circle. Also a bit of a polymath, he's an ex-Big Four auditor and now the plaid-shirted king of Antipodean dude food, known for uber-popular Surry Hills joints Hoe Dawg and Douchely. I ask Lee about his love of French–Japanese fusion hot dogs and cold drip espresso martinis, his worship of nose-to-tail chefs and craft beer artisans.

'Man, you've done your homework on me,' he says. 'The Capote of the food world, hey?'

I tell him I keep my ear to the ground.

I ask Lee what he thinks of G. He credits him as an inspiration.

'What we're seeing in Bart's work is mind-blowing, to say the least,' says Lee. 'He's the go-to guy for innovation. An absolute revelation. Everyone who's anyone worships him. He's ice-cream royalty, and no one's going to get anywhere near him for a very long time.'

'Ready to see where the magic happens?' says G. He presses a button on a remote. The security gates swing open.

G's house is a glass hemisphere – a stand-out look for the industrial Alexandria skyline.

'It's a converted warehouse,' he says as we walk up the driveway. 'I told my architect to design me a place that literally looks like the Sydney housing bubble.'

On the front steps, we run into G's advertising team. He has them living on the premises while they develop the promotional strategy for the venture. They're standing around in a cloud of their own herbal smoke, holding their cigarettes out to the side, tapping the ash. They are in the midst of an impenetrable conversation about organic Dutch carrots and *mise en scène* and style sins and intercultural artistic collectives.

G introduces me to the art director. 'Tell her about the campaign, Rhys.'

Rhys visibly shivers with excitement under his Native American headdress. 'Oh my God, it's so high concept it's on Pluto. It's so underground it's above ground.'

I tell him I'm very curious about the new product.

'Hells yeah,' says Rhys. 'So are we.'

He doesn't even know what the product is?

'Well, no. But we'd totes line up to taste it. We hear it's a killer flavour.'

In the hallway we have to edge past a TV crew.

'Just ignore them,' says G. 'They're filming our renovation contest.'

The hallway leads us straight through to the centre of the bubble. The ceiling, at its highest point, must be ten metres above the floor.

'Money comes, money goes,' says G. 'You have to do something with it. May as well be high ceilings.'

In the centre of the bubble is a circular pool area with two yellow slippery slides. The slide on the left is open-topped. The slide on the right is a closed tunnel. Two streams of beautiful naked women with high hair and big breasts slide down them over and over again. The accompanying soundscape seems to be a recording of a busy construction site.

'Like it?' asks G. 'It's an art installation. You have two viewing options. You can either watch the ladies slide all the way down on the left, or on the right you can delay visual gratification until they pop out the end. The fact that I buy important pieces of art like this, it really makes me feel like I'm giving back to the community – completing the loop.'

Lining the outer area of the bubble are rooms with views of the central pool.

G shows us the kitchen first, where a pair of eager contestants is awaiting G's approval. G casts his eye over the space – which is scattered with multicoloured Eames chairs – and shakes his head.

'The splashback has to go,' he says. 'What were you thinking? Three out of ten.'

We move on with the TV crew. Pairs of contestants have been assigned to each room. The boom operator tells me that each couple is responsible for renovating a room according to a theme selected by G. The money comes out of their own pockets, with many contestants borrowing against their own homes.

Most are in a state of panic. They stand in the middle of their rooms, heads bowed, weeping silently, with paint rollers in their hands. A rumour is going around that the team with the lowest score at the end of the day will be asked to crawl out of the bubble on their hands and knees, before being whisked off to an hour-long session of electroshock therapy.

I ask what the show is called.

'Is it a show? We hired a camera crew, so I guess it looks like a show. I just wanted a reno, really. The original interior was so last quarter.'

What's in it for the contestants?

'Potential exposure.'

G takes us through to his bedroom, which is dominated by a custom calf-leather bed shaped like a waxed vagina.

'I adore this piece because it goes right to the heart of the question: "Can art be commercial?" You have to sleep right in the centre of it, though, to be comfortable. Or you'll roll over the edges.'

On the wall is a framed spread he did for a *Good Weekend* interview. It shows him curled in foetal position in the middle of the bed.

'Someone told me it's outrageous, like sleeping in a little girl's fanny.' He shrugs. 'Taste. You either have it or you don't.'

Out the back of the property is where all the real action is taking place. Connected to the main bubble by a glass walkway is a smaller bubble housing G's experimental kitchen headquarters, a veritable temple for the worship of the ice-cream gods.

There is all manner of stainless steel equipment. G's crew – in chef's whites, hair nets, face masks and gloves – is cooking up a storm. They're hard at work bringing in trays of eggs, grating orange zest, shelling Sicilian pistachios, weighing saffron, unwrapping parcels of camembert, and slicing open vanilla pods.

As part of what G calls his Multi-sensorial Method, the team listens to a mix of nature soundtracks and Sigur Rós while concocting new flavours to add to the more than 220 already in G's arsenal.

G has built his reputation on making seemingly impossible taste combinations work in complete harmony. Some have dubbed him the bad boy of ice-cream for attempting these edible highwire acts – madness for the tastebuds. One of his most popular flavours is sage, roast duck and single-origin cardboard.

'For that one we had to get the balance perfectly right,' says G. 'We had to keep in mind that the duck was the hero of the ice-cream, and things went smoothly from there.'

G takes me over to a Carpigiani batch freezer, which is in the process of discharging newly frozen duck ice-cream. One of his assistants is collecting the ice-cream from the machine in a stainless steel pan, helping it along with a spatula. G dips a wooden popsicle stick into the pan and hands it to me.

'Give it a try. We've just switched to organic bullock milk for this flavour.'

The ice-cream has a full-bodied, creamy mouthfeel unlike any other I've tasted. The duck is surprisingly punchy and unapologetic.

Next, G opens a round metal tin for me. 'Smell this. The rarest tea in the world. It's made of soft down plucked from the pubic region of virgins and folded into twenty-four-carat gold dust. I use it in the Virginal – the most expensive ice-cream in our range.' He runs his pinkie along the inside of the tin lid and shows me the tip, now covered in fine gold. 'You can use it as make-up too.'

The Virginal will set customers back a cool $1,000. It comes in G's signature waffle cone, which is coated in dark chocolate and freeze-dried coffee granules. 'The coffee adds an extra crunchy element to the overall ice-cream,' adds G.

For those who have less cash kicking around in their bank accounts, there is the Aspirational – half the price and made from Tahitian vanilla combined with the essence of Giza 45, the most highly graded Egyptian cotton.

I laughingly ask if G has gone so far as to use drugs in his cones.

'Look, everyone's done a weed cone,' he says. 'That fad's over. We've been experimenting with a new substance for today's venture – a secret ingredient that, fingers crossed, will pay massive dividends.'

He points to one of his assistants, who is opening a cardboard box with a Stanley knife.

'That's a new shipment of it.'

I wander over and peer at the address on the box. The ingredient appears to be sourced from Bolivia.

'Come on,' says G. 'Let's get this show on the road.'

G takes me out to the street in front of the housing bubble.

A van is now parked there. It's matt black except for the words *Cream Reaper* painted in white cursive lettering on the front and side.

'We're moving into ice-cream vans,' says G. 'This is my new extreme pop-up concept. We're launching the trial today in Surry Hills. If we're successful, we'll expand the fleet.'

'Where's the menu?' I ask. 'Isn't it usually on the side of the van?'

'No need. There's only one flavour.' He gets into the driver's seat. 'Hop in.'

He reaches out through the window and pulls a rope. A bell clangs. 'I hate "Greensleeves",' he explains.

As we pull out of the property, we chat about the new venture.

'It's all good to be making beautiful ice-creams and to be turning that into a sustainable business,' says G, 'but I need to be thinking strategically. The thing is, you always have to think of what you need to do to stay ahead of the competition. That's the nature of business. If you've ever owned a cafe, you'd know how it is. You're always checking out the menus of your competitors, seeing if you can do better for a particular price point, shifting your menu to keep up with food trends. If a competitor does a deconstructed eggs Benedict, you do a *reconstructed* deconstructed eggs Benedict. When it comes to the ice-cream business, how do you stay miles ahead of the rest – escape the daily tit-for-tat? You gotta be streetwise, you know, meaning you have to know what they want on the streets. You need more than just a high-concept ice-cream. You need a game changer. And what do you think the game changer is?'

Buy one get one free, I suggest.

'I saw this Instagram post, right? And this girl wrote that she would, and I quote, *kill* for one of my ice-creams and I thought, as I slid down the left slippery slide, I wonder if she would literally *die* for one. That's a gap in the market if I ever spied one. What if I decided to take ice-cream out of the ice-cream business and turn it into an extreme sport? What if an ice-cream existed that said to foodies every-where: "How serious are you about food?" An ice-cream that sorts the professionals from the amateurs, the men from the boys. So I thought I'd put the word out. Call in the media. We're going to try it out today.'

The first customer to front up to the van is Elena1995, an artificial redhead with a perfect French manicure.

She has volunteered to debut the product. She's been informed in advance of its ingredients and has signed a confidentiality agreement not to disclose the information prior to today.

Her Instagram bio says she's a *blogger, food fashionista, shutterbug, media darling, style guru, real estate maven, NYU Art History major, emerging curator, mag hag, cake pop addict, daddy's little sophisticate, 22. Sydney via NY & San Fran. Good hair or go home.*

'I want two,' Elena1995 says to G. 'One for the money shot and another as backup.'

G gets to work. He pushes down a lever on a machine and makes a soft serve cone. He dips it in chocolate and pushes a Flake into the side. It looks like a regular cone from a regular ice-cream van. It's nothing like the concoctions I've seen in the lab.

He hands the cone to Elena1995 through the window.

She makes a face.

I ask her what's wrong.

'If this is meant to be an extreme ice-cream,' she tells me, 'it could at least be visually marketable. Like, add something that makes it pop.'

'Do you want it or not?' says G.

'Whatevs.' She pulls out a gold-plated ice-cream stand and sets it on the counter. She snaps the ice-cream from thirty different angles with her phone. She walks away playing with the filters.

I ask G what makes the product so extreme.

'The concept is: you put down the cash for it, we give you an ice-cream that has a fifty per cent chance of killing you on the spot.'

A lethal ice-cream?

'Absolutely,' he says. 'There's so much theatre to this product. I love it. The secret ingredient in it has this knockout deliciousness – a devastating flavour that I can guarantee you no one in the world has tasted. It may even be an as-yet-undiscovered basic taste – way more complex than umami. But the catch is that once you've tasted it, you may have to die. It's just the nature of the ingredient.

More addictive than sugar, too, so anyone who survives is going to be a repeat customer. This ice-cream's worth more than the rest of my business combined. This is the magic fucking bullet.'

I suggest that perhaps the whole scheme isn't actually legal.

'Look,' says G, 'if one had to come down on the side of legality or illegality, the side one would land on would most likely be illegality. But, you know, it doesn't leave a trace. Plus, it's a highly regulated scheme. Ian will be doing regular audits to check that it truly is a fifty-fifty chance for each customer. That we're not tampering with the odds. Hey, Ian, you're still here, right?'

Lee pops out of nowhere, brandishing a green pen.

Elena1995 sashays back.

'Pro tip for your food article,' she says to me. 'If you put the whites in the photos up really high, like, it looks like everything's literally bathed in light.'

She has uploaded the photo to Instagram. She shows me the post. The caption reads:

#allthegoodness #nomnomnom #ultimatefoodie #foodporn #dedicationtocraft #icecreamordeath #seeyouontheothersidemaybe #loveallmybesties #hugz #hashtagitsabiatchlife #idie

The ice-cream is melting on its stand. Rivulets of white snake their way down the cone.

'Ew.' She takes the cone and tosses it onto the road.

G hands her the backup cone.

She sits on the kerb and goes quiet. The whole street is quiet: no one else is around. She eats the ice-cream, nibbling on it like a tiny rabbit. She has her phone in one hand and stares at the likes piling up on Instagram.

I exit the van and sit down next to her.

How does it taste?

'No words.'

How is she feeling?

She shows me her phone. 'All the love!'

I mean, is she feeling ill?

'I've got the luck of the Irish. It's, like, in the family or something. I'm hardly going to die from an ice-cream.'

A minute later, she's doing the hippy shakes on the ground, eyeballs rolling, saliva bubbling from the lips.

Her body comes to a complete standstill. Her limbs have settled at weird angles. The hem of her dress has hiked up to her waist, exposing frilly white briefs with pink spots.

The hand holding the phone is outstretched. The likes keep piling up on Instagram.

I put two fingers on her neck.

There isn't a pulse.

I ask G what he's going to do.

G sighs. 'It's pretty dull isn't it, the experience? We might have to develop add-ons – offer a more attractive package. Get them to bring a USB stick with their photos and literally flash their memories before their eyes. Play their favourite James Blunt single.'

He pours unpasteurised honey from a large pail into a smaller pail. It spills in slow motion. I ask him what he's doing.

'It helps me think.'

I ask him again what he's going to do about the body. Surely he's not going to leave corpses strewn around the city like a trail of breadcrumbs?

'I guess it *is* substandard customer care. A bad look for the brand, probably.'

G continues to pour the honey for a good few minutes. As he does so, it becomes apparent to me that this feature article could end prematurely with the subject pouring honey from one container to another for no practical reason. I wonder out loud what other embedded journalists do in these situations. Do they get involved?

I make a decision.

I tell G I'm curious to see where this goes, even if it gets me in trouble. In fact, I know someone who may be able to help out. The stepmother of a primary school friend of mine drives a transfer van that collects dead bodies from hospitals and homes, and takes them to funeral parlours.

'Sounds good,' says G.

But where should she take the body?

'The morgue or something?'

I tell him he'll get arrested.

G comes out of the van. He looks at the body, then at me.

'Look,' he says, 'so I didn't give much thought to corpse disposal. But I've had some quiet discussions with various councils and they're happy for my permits to incorporate a small population cull. The whole city's overpopulated, so it's good from a public health perspective. Plus it's a more palatable death experience. If they did it with garbage trucks, it wouldn't be as good, would it? And if you're stupid enough to buy a Reaper, then you deserve to die. It's natural selection. It's a self-selecting cull.'

I find it difficult to believe this permit arrangement exists.

'I put a little grease in the wheels of government,' G says, 'and they turned for me. And the police are always happy to close one eye in return for free product. It's a cut-throat industry. People call me the bad boy of Sydney ice-cream, but I don't think they know what bad boy really means. It's a fucking war out there, lady. And I intend to win it with ice-cream.'

Mrs Tracey arrives in her white Toyota HiAce.

She is dressed to match her van, in a loose tux-style white shirt with the sleeves pushed up just past her wrists. She is wearing tailored white pants, white flats and pearl earrings.

'I just came from a fantastically good lunch with some of the mothers from my grandson's playgroup,' she says. 'You know that new place everyone's raving about that does the toffee offal?'

G shakes her hand. He explains what has transpired and asks if she can take the body to a hospital and tell them she found the blogger lying in the street, on the verge of death.

As they talk, I reminisce. In primary school, Mrs Tracey was always one of those nice mothers who brought Tupperware containers full of sliced oranges to our netball games for the half-time break. She was one of those women who was so positive and wide-eyed about everything that you might have thought she'd been slammed in the head by a wayward crane.

Even now, as she talks to G, she nods understandingly, giving him those wide eyes. It's from her training in the death-care industry. She smiles with that big red-lipsticked

83

overbite in such an empty way that it seems she might not even realise the gravity of the situation. If you sliced off the top of her head and looked in, it'd probably be full of mist and red carnations and rectangular wholesale wake cakes in chocolate and orange poppyseed, and a pasty organist playing 'Make Me a Channel of Your Peace'.

We all stare at the former Elena1995.

'I picked up three bodies this morning on the way to lunch,' says Mrs Tracey. 'So I have one more bed for your girl. Serendipity.'

She straps Elena1995 into a stretcher and loads her into the back of the van.

'Would you mind very much if we take a photo together?' Mrs Tracey asks G. 'I'm just so thrilled to meet such a famous artisan ice-cream maker.'

'An odd time for a photo,' says Lee, as we cluster together.

'Say cheese,' says Mrs Tracey.

Mrs Tracey drops me home before she drops off the bodies.

'What *is* this?' she says. 'A hole in the wall?'

It literally is. It's one of the thousands of new horizontal hovels the city has recently listed on a special register to address the housing crisis. If you earn under $40,000 per year, you qualify to rent one of these holes for a subsidised rate of $750 a week. The initiative was inspired by the Japanese capsule-hotel concept except that the holes aren't capsules, just concrete tubes with open ends.

'It comes with a postbox,' I tell her.

'Dear girl,' says Mrs Tracey, 'you must start making more money.'

As Mrs Tracey drives off, I make diving hands and launch myself into the hole.

I light a match and hold it up to the fire sprinkler to set it off so I can wash my face.

All refreshed for a night in, I lie in my horizontal hole eating a deluxe muesli bar from ALDI and fall asleep pondering the mechanics of G's rapid ascent through the frozen-food ranks.

The next morning, Mrs Tracey unexpectedly shows up again in her white HiAce.

From the back window of G's van, I spot her in the distance trailing us. When the van stops, she stops.

G knocks out a few Cream Reapers in the morning and, each time, the very second that the hand with the smartphone flops out on the pavement, Mrs Tracey is there to pick up the body and load it into her van.

It's a slick operation.

She carries the bodies all by herself, slinging them over her shoulder and dumping them on the stretchers. She has a strange level of upper body strength, especially for someone built like an English rose.

I follow G out to see her. I warn Mrs Tracey that she shouldn't get involved.

'You suggested it, my dear.'

G laughs. 'Looks as if Mrs Tracey has a better business mind than you.'

'It's undeniably a growth industry,' says Mrs Tracey. 'You can smell the desperation out there. But you can't cart all your customers off to hospital. It'd be better for you if these people just go missing, and I can help with that.'

G invites her into his van for a private conversation.

Mrs Tracey and her HiAce are hired on a permanent basis, with key performance targets based on numbers of bodies transported. In fact, G hires all of the lady drivers comprising the Tracey's Transportables workforce. He shouts the team to a lavish toffee-offal brunch and woos them with the promise that he will buy them a brand spanking new fleet of white Toyota HiAces and have each vehicle fitted out with a stunning four-bed interior.

With Mrs Tracey's team on board, G decides it's time to expand the Cream Reaper fleet. Nine more black vans set out across Sydney, each trailed at a respectable distance by a HiAce complete with lady driver. The rest of Mrs Tracey's ladies are assigned to backup vans, on call to take over body collection duties when the designated HiAces are at capacity. The cost of running the transfer vans is incorporated into the price of the Cream Reaper ice-cream packages.

I am curious about where Mrs Tracey intends to take the increasing number of bodies.

'I'm a woman with connections. I know people who can disappear people, in return for a cut of my fee. I'm an expert in unpublicity.'

Lee is sceptical that anyone can be disappeared.

'If you think things can't be hidden in Sydney,' Mrs Tracey tells him, 'you're reading the wrong news.'

Mrs Tracey decides to embark on a more active role in the operation. She takes to stepping out of her HiAce to 'stretch her legs', hovering around our van and keeping an eye out for potential customers.

'I have a performance target, after all,' she says.

In Double Bay, she goes for a short walk and returns steering a middle-aged woman by the elbow. The woman is wearing head-to-toe beige and has just had a facial. With no make-up on, she squints out at us from behind dark glasses.

'It's over,' says the woman. 'It's over, it's over, it's over, it's over.' She has a crisp, newsreader's voice. She refuses to elaborate.

She calls her lawyer. 'Yes, of course it's Elizabeth. Don't you know my voice? Just make sure the yacht goes to Chalice. No, I'm not in the bathtub, I don't have pills, I'm eating *ice-cream*, for God's sake. I'm fucking *celebrating* life.'

The ice-cream, however, doesn't kill her.

'My God, that's delicious,' she says to G, 'give me another one.' She pulls an Amex out of a crocodile-leather purse and slaps it on the counter. 'Use this until I'm done.'

Nothing happens after the second ice-cream.

She orders more.

She sits on the grass median strip eating one ice-cream after another.

Customers come and go. As they line up, they glance periodically at this gaunt expensive woman pushing ice-creams into her face.

She turns to glare at them, mouth smeared white.

'Fuck the whole business,' she says.

I ask her if she means the entirety of a particular registered business, or life in general.

'Fuck your mother.'

The sun begins to set. Orange moves into blue, and the six or so cones still haven't killed her.

'You know what, darling?' she says to me. 'I'm lactose intolerant.'

She pushes an index finger into her throat, and throws up. She throws up on the grass, on the road, on her own trousers. The puke is somehow beige.

'There, there,' says Mrs Tracey, hurrying over, patting her on the shoulder. 'Someone needs a little rest.'

In an instant, Mrs Tracey has stabbed her with a needle, strapped her into a stretcher, loaded her into the back of the HiAce and driven off.

By Wednesday, Mrs Tracey has designed a $4.99 Cream Reaper app downloadable to smartphones.

She gives a demonstration to G and Lee.

'This transforms the venture into an on-demand service. You press this button to request a cone. You enter your location. If you select "Deliver Now", the closest van will respond to the request. When the van is within a kilometre of your location, you can watch it move towards you on a map. Alternatively, you can choose a date from this calendar so there's time to get your affairs in order in case you end up dying.'

G agrees to trial it.

For most of the day, no requests come in. Lee wonders out loud if the app actually works. Mrs Tracey gives him the finger behind his back.

Near midnight, just as the shift is about to end, the first request comes in. Ten ice-creams to be delivered to the forecourt of the Museum of Sydney.

We arrive to discover a handful of drunk young suits playing parkour.

Two short ones have clambered onto the sandstone wall of the museum cafe and are taking bets on who can jump the furthest from it. The only perceivable difference between the two is that one is wearing a red tie with blue stripes, and the other is wearing a blue tie with red stripes.

'Three hundred says Murphy's going to win by a metre.'

'I'm putting four on Babiak. Look at those legs!'

Someone wolf whistles. They laugh.

G leans out of the van. 'You called?'

'Ah, fuck!' shouts Red Tie. He checks his watch and looks at G. 'You got here before twelve.'

Blue Tie laughs and mimes a basketball shot. 'That's a cool hundred, right there, Jimmy boy. Two fiddys, mate.'

Red Tie gets out his wallet and hands over the notes.

They get off the wall and follow the others to the van. Their breath reeks of beer.

'What's going down this fine evening, gentlemen?' says G.

'Put a few away at The 'Stab,' says Red Tie. He shoves Blue Tie. 'It's this guy's birthday. Took his wedding ring off to celebrate. Chatted up some of the ladies.'

Mrs Tracey, hovering again, asks them what they do for work.

Red Tie whips out business cards. 'We're institutional banking analysts. For all your institutional banking needs.'

G looks at the name on the card. He takes us aside. 'He's the brother of one of my suppliers. Can't sell them the cones.'

'Are you kidding?' says Mrs Tracey. 'No kills?'

'I'm giving them plain vanilla. They won't know the difference.'

Mrs Tracey goes red in the face. 'No one wastes my time.'

She turns to the bankers and tells them there's an extra charge of three grand each for a tasteful, though modest, pre-paid funeral should they experience death by Cream Reaper. She holds out her hand for their credit cards.

'That's a bit much,' says Red Tie.

'Didn't realise you were cheap,' says Mrs Tracey.

'Ooh,' say the other bankers. 'Burn!'

Red Tie surrenders his credit card. The others follow.

G hands out plain vanilla cones. The bankers stand in a circle nudging each other and laughing, making bets on who's going to drop dead first.

Ten minutes later, they're still standing.

Now that they've tried the best taste in the world, they declare that it's pretty shit after all. But it dawns on them that they've just been given a second chance at life. The hairs on the backs of their necks stand up. They feel all-powerful. Their senses are heightened. They were meant to live!

They run back to the sandstone wall and start taking more bets.

I get into Mrs Tracey's van for a lift home.

As we drive off, I look back at the bankers. Red Tie has jumped further than Blue Tie, and is rolling around on the ground in pain, clutching a broken foot.

'Little superdicks,' says Mrs Tracey, wiping the app from their phones remotely.

We are gods of the streets. Winners of the ice-cream war.

Our bells clang through the suburbs of Sydney.

Mrs Tracey never flags, picking up the bodies one by one as they slump over front gates and garden gnomes and azalea bushes.

Drivers of pink and white ice-cream vans give us the finger as we cruise past.

'That's all you got?' G yells.

No one can touch us.

We're putting them out of business.

We have so many customers that Mrs Tracey starts to help out in the main van.

A girl in Strathfield Square brings along her date, who loiters ten feet from the van.

'I'm so boring,' she whispers to Mrs Tracey, almost in tears. 'He keeps checking his Instagram feed instead of talking to me. He'd prefer to see a stream of amateur cat pictures than my ugly face. I don't know how to make myself more interesting. I thought he might like an ice-cream. I mean, everyone says this is an extreme sport.'

Taking two cones from Mrs Tracey, the girl gives one to the guy, who is still snorting at the funny posts on his phone. He holds his hand out for the cone without looking up.

Soon he's on the ground, seizing up. The girl is left standing.

'Good luck with the dating,' says Mrs Tracey.

Mrs Tracey has a new surveillance operation going with some of the ladies, who have come into G's flagship van to show us how it works.

'We intercept calls, texts and emails in the general vicinity. The system has keyword triggers in place that alert us to the relevant location.'

'What sort of words?' asks G. 'Suicidal ones?'

'That's not interesting to us.'

The surveillance equipment beeps. A map flicks up on Mrs Tracey's laptop that indicates we should try our luck at the Paddington Reservoir Gardens.

'Time for a joy kill,' says Mrs Tracey, with an alarming coldness in her voice.

We come upon a young man in boat shoes, lying in the grass of the sunken garden, staring at the brick arches and penning a travel article about the radical self-expression and transcendent beauty of Burning Man.

I serve him a Reaper and ask how he is.

'I'm so tortured,' he says as he takes his first lick. 'I'm such a tortured, tortured writer. So, so tortured. So very much tortured. In this article I'm breaking apart the genre of creative non-fiction, I'm writing the sparest of spare sentences that never ends, I'm wanking, wanking so hard over myself, I can't even write a paragraph without wanking, I'm wanking simultaneously with all the other boys in our wanky boys' club, we're all seeing who can wank the hardest, who can write the wankiest glowing reviews of our friends' work, and our cum shoots out in grand arcs over every page – can't you see all the cum on the page? – and after this I'm going to write a book that's a cross between *Ulysses* and Hemingway and Franzen, the next big black story of redemption, who cares if I'm white, it's going to be the greatest bunch of wank with the wankiest fucking climax, oh my God, oh my fucking God, it feels so good, I'm going to come, ah, ah, I'm coming now, ah, aaaaaaaahh.'

He groans. Turns cold. Mrs Tracey shoves him into the back of the van and slams the door.

She gives me a look.

'For crying out loud,' she says, 'don't ask them how they are.'

Word is spreading. Business is skyrocketing. It's the last day of the assignment and I don't want it to end.

Our bells toll through the night. People who hear us start to shit themselves like little Pavlovian dogs.

We top off a surprising number of customers. Hedge-fund managers in polo shirts, kicking back after twilight sailing at Rushcutters Bay. Idiot kids trailing us in their P plates, egging each other on. A tradie being ushered out of BBQ King for trying to start a brawl. A bankrupt restaurateur, smoking in an alley, trying to figure out how to tell his staff he can't pay their overdue superannuation entitlements.

'That was a good crowd,' says Mrs Tracey at the end of the shift. She claps G on the shoulder. 'Your next step is to narrow your whole ice-cream range down to this one flavour. This is the money spinner.'

G isn't so sure anymore. 'I'm an artist,' he tells Mrs Tracey. 'I wasn't born to make just one flavour. The speed of this expansion is denigrating the artistic sensibilities of my work. I don't like it.'

'Think bolder,' says Mrs Tracey. 'Stay ahead of the

pack. Where are your balls? Did you lose them in a lake somewhere?'

'Stop trying to take over my business,' says G. 'Back down, bitch!'

G and Lee retire to the van to debrief on the week that was.

I hear them whispering. They're panicking that the situation is out of hand.

'I told you an embedded journalist was a bad idea,' Lee is saying. 'You can't invite press to cover the trial of a semi-illegal product. And now you've got this old woman, one Hush Puppy in the grave, trying to take over.'

'You're right,' says G, resting his forehead on the steering wheel.

'What newspaper is she from, that journalist?'

G shrugs. 'A major one?'

'You know what we're going to have to do,' says Lee, writing something on his clipboard with his green pen. 'It's not going to be pleasant.'

G leans over and looks at the clipboard.

They turn and look at me through the clear window panel.

In the early hours of the morning, I am lying in my hovel licking peanut butter off a tablespoon when I hear the bell tolling.

Death is coming to collect me.

It draws closer and closer, rolling up to my hole in the wall.

G and Lee step out of the van. Mrs Tracey's HiAce draws up behind them. She must have given them my address. She shrugs at me from the driver's seat of her HiAce.

I ask them if they're here to do me in.

'Quite the opposite,' says G. 'We thought we'd bring you into the fold. How about it? You agree not to publish the article, you keep your mouth shut, you pocket a third of the profits. But the old bird has to go.'

I tell them it sounds like a plan. We shake hands.

I'm excited. I tell them how inspired I've been by their work. How I've been working on a new flavour I'd like them to try.

'I can't guarantee it will make it onto the menu,' says G.

I wriggle into my concrete hole and wriggle back out with two scoops of my new concoction.

They take one lick, then a second.

'Not bad,' says G, 'for a journalist.'

Lee nods. 'There's a flavour in it I can't identify.'

G smiles. 'Our little prodigy is innovating already.'

One minute later, he's fritzing on the ground.

Two minutes later, Lee joins him.

They stare up at me, ice-cream dribbling from their mouths.

'I'm calling this one the Magic Bullet,' I say. 'It has a one hundred per cent kill rate.'

G curls up in pain. 'Who *are* you?' he shrieks.

'Good of you to ask. I'm a staff writer at *Gastronomob*. The article I'm writing is: "How to Execute a Hostile Takeover in One Working Week". You guys think I'm the Capote of the food world? I'd say I'm more the Capone.'

A couple more spasms and they're dead.

'Business,' I say, standing over the bodies. 'You either get it or you don't.'

'They never learn, do they?' says Mrs Tracey. 'Always leave death to the professionals.' She hands over a USB stick. 'Photos for the article.'

I wink at her. 'We're all set, then.'

Mrs Tracey wheels the bodies into the back of the HiAce.

We get in the front.

'Where to, boss?'

I notice the sun is beginning to rise. 'Let's see where the morning takes us.'

The surveillance system beeps, alerting us to three stray uses of '*mise en scène*'. A map flashes up, pinpointing a familiar location.

'Want to check out some new digs, Mrs Tracey?'

The hipsters hear the tolling of the bell. They wander out in their pyjamas through the front gates of the housing bubble.

'Killer ice-cream for breakfast,' they yawn. 'Hells yeah.'

The Three-Dimensional
Yellow Man

It was only when a one-dimensional yellow man stepped out of a cinema screen and into a plush red theatre on George Street that audience members noticed him from behind their 3D glasses.

The film from which the man had emerged was *Return of the White Ninja 3D*. Although the film was in 3D, the yellow man only appeared in 1D. He had been playing Stand-offish Ninja #13, part of a gang of 1D Stand-offish Ninjas led by a 3D white boy who had been raised by ninjas from birth.

In the middle of the closing scene, in which the ninjas had formed a circle and were bowing to the white boy with new-found respect, Stand-offish Ninja #13 had glimpsed light from the movie projector falling onto the heads of the audience. Curious, he had stepped towards the light and into the lap of a blond-haired woman – one foot landing in her supersized popcorn and the other on the spare seat beside her.

The newly three-dimensional yellow man stretched his limbs and tossed his hair. The audience gasped. He had a luminescent quality about him, having just stepped out of a celluloid dream.

He looked around.

Maybe life will be better, he thought, *in three dimensions.*

At first, the cinemagoers were calm. They shook his hand, starstruck, because they assumed he was a white actor doing yellow face. They thought his slit eyes, flat nose and jet black hair were the work of a good make-up artist.

But when the man shed his ninja costume, strolled out into the foyer and began walking the streets of the island naked, they saw that he was yellow all over.

This could not just have been make-up, they concluded, because he had been clothed in the scene he had exited. There would not have been, from a filmmaking perspective, any practical need to paint the balls of a white actor yellow.

Realising that an actual yellow ninja was on the loose, the cinemagoers started screaming in horror.

The yellow man cleared his three-dimensional throat and began to speak.

The first word that came out was *Fellini.*

Incredible, he thought, *I have a three-dimensional vocabulary.*

He had previously grunted and roundhouse kicked his way through films, his only two speaking lines being: *You die now* and *Boss Man velly angly.*

The yellow man acquired a smart jacket and trousers. He decided that, with his new-found dimensions, he would spend his time on intellectual pursuits, with a focus on the study of the representation of women in Italian neorealist cinema.

The yellow man wrote a book on the subject. Consequently, he was invited to participate in a panel discussion at one of the island's arts festivals. The other selected panellists were also yellow men, who were visiting from abroad to promote books they had written on diverse topics such as Olympic shot-put and the history of chemical warfare.

What is it like to be yellow? asked the interviewer of the yellow man.

That's not the only thing I'm interested in talking about, he replied. *After all, the book I've written is about Federico Fellini and how women are represented in his films.*

I see, said the interviewer. *But how has your yellowness impacted on your work? For instance, have you ever thought of forming a Yellow Man Group, similar to America's iconic Blue Man Group?*

With my fellow panellists? asked the yellow man. *No, that hasn't crossed my mind, particularly since this is the first time we've all met.*

It'd be quite a novelty, though, said the interviewer.

Would it? asked the yellow man.

Being yellow yourself, continued the interviewer, *why are you not writing about being yellow?*

Because I wanted to write about Italian neorealism, said the yellow man.

A long silence filled the auditorium.

The yellow man sighed.

Do you really want to know what it's like to be yellow?

The interviewer nodded.

Well, said the yellow man. He crossed his legs, clasped his hands together and rested them on one knee. *Being yellow is like being the colour of sunflowers, or of lemons, or of pretty yellow ribbons in the hair of a young girl. It's like being the colour of a dishwashing detergent labelled with a picture of the morning sun bursting through the kitchen window and alighting on a gleaming, freshly washed wine glass.*

How fascinating, said the interviewer.

It is quite an interesting colour to be, nodded the yellow man, *and it is, I believe, a hue that is somewhere on the colour wheel between green and orange.*

My God, he can speak English well, murmured members of the audience. *And without any sort of accent.*

Yellowness, continued the man, *gives one a certain je ne sais quoi.*

My God, they thought. *He's speaking European. These yellows can blend in when they put their minds to it.*

I've been wondering, said the interviewer, *about the faraway places where all the yellow people come from. Why is it that I'm so afraid of going there?*

That's something for you to work out with your therapist, said the yellow man. He turned to the audience. *For those of you interested in my next book,* he said, *I will be embarking on a study of Shakespeare and debt, with a focus on* The Merchant of Venice.

Many of the audience members, as they left the auditorium, wondered why he had to be so argumentative.

Prickly, they muttered to each other. *Inscrutable.*

★

While the panel discussion was taking place, reports filtered in from around the island that a naked three-dimensional yellow woman had burst out from the very same cinema screen on George Street.

She, too, had noticed the light beaming from the movie projector while in the middle of playing a 1D character in a 3D biopic. This, her breakthrough role – as the unhinged, manipulative, gold-digging girlfriend of a white social-networking entrepreneur – had been invented by the screenwriters to serve as a plot device. Her character's primary purpose in the film was to heighten conflict in a climactic scene in which a hand-held camera followed the entrepreneur as he pleaded into his phone in an attempt to save an ailing business partnership, while she – experiencing a psychotic episode – lured him into a hotel room, locked the door, stripped naked and set the curtains on fire.

This had been her most three-dimensional one-dimensional role to date. Prior to this, her roles had been non-speaking ones – her specialty being silent waitresses and whores. She had also once played a dragon lady whose long, straight hair curled around the necks of men and strangled them in their sleep.

As the yellow woman walked out of the flames and onto the street, men bumped past her as if she were invisible. Others stopped and stared.

Ni hao, they said. *Konnichiwa.*

Bonjour, she replied. *Guten Tag.*

When she took men home, they said, *I've never tried a yellow girl before.*

They ran their hands up and down her limbs and across her stomach.

My God, they said, *I'd heard yellow girls have smooth skin.*

They cupped her breasts in their hands as if weighing them.

You've got big breasts for a yellow girl, they said. *Because that's a problem for yellows. I mean, not really a problem but ... breast size is an issue.*

I have a beautiful brain, said the yellow woman. *One day I'll be a highly regarded public intellectual.*

That's nice, said the men, pushing her head down. *Do that amazing thing you do with your tongue.*

I didn't even realise I was yellow, said the woman, sweeping aside books on Rawlsian liberalism to make room for the men. *I thought I had blue eyes.*

Be grateful, the men said. *You can't have everything.*

★

Soon after the yellow man and yellow woman stepped out of the cinema, their kind began to multiply.

It was not difficult to ascertain the origin of these new yellow arrivals. A few were escaping gold-rush dramedies but the majority had been playing non-English speaking Illegal Fishermen #1 to #2,873 in a high-rating border protection TV series. They began to jump out of leaky boats from TV screens and into lounge rooms, shaking their hair and limbs as if reborn.

The yellow people took over whole shopping arcades with their cut-price electronics and two-dollar shops, their food outlets with the dead ducks hung up on hooks in the windows, and their grocery stores with racks of strange-looking vegetables that looked like weeds.

Human Resources departments implemented Non-Discrimination and Equal Opportunity policies while quietly passing over job applications that featured yellow-sounding names, unless the candidates in question exhibited sufficient assimilation, demonstrated outstanding academic achievement, and/or were photogenic enough to be in corporate brochures that highlighted the cultural diversity of personnel.

Whenever the yellow woman found herself stuck in a train with a crowd dominated by yellow people, she would make a point of speaking louder than usual on her phone. Taking pains to converse in the local accent with the person on the other end of the line, she sought to emphasise to the few white people within earshot that at least one yellow person in the carriage had bothered to master the native language of the island.

This demonstration of her successful integration would always please her initially, then make her feel sick.

In the end, she stopped speaking altogether.

*

By this point, locals all around the island were panicking at the unprecedented influx of yellow people. The yellows were beginning to amass cash – probably through drug deals – to buy houses in white neighbourhoods. They were infiltrating schools, universities and white-collar workplaces.

It was getting worse than a zombie invasion. The yellows

walked like automatons down the street, overpowering people with their kimchi breath.

I can't tell the difference between any of them, some shouted.

Their yellowness is blinding like the sun, others screamed, clawing at their eyes.

Commentators blamed the first yellow man. He had failed to warn them that yellow people could be yellow like the sun. He had only said that they were yellow like pretty ribbons in the hair of a little girl.

Out of a fish and chip shop appeared a tight-lipped, flame-haired woman.

I don't like it, she said. *We're in danger of being swamped by yellows. They stick to themselves and form ghettos. They're stealing our jobs. Political correctness is ruining our island. Please explain*, she said, because she really didn't understand.

The flame-haired woman became an island-wide sensation. She was offered a spot on a local TV show in which celebrities performed routines such as the foxtrot and tango, and were voted off according to public opinion.

In a paso doble, the flame-haired woman was dragged awkwardly across the dance floor by the chief of the island, a little frog-mouthed man with thick eyebrows, who was dressed as a bullfighter.

The crowd cheered. The punters at home texted her name each week to keep her in the competition.

She's a bit of all right, they thought, watching from pubs and couches as she was awarded runner-up.

★

Unwilling to bend to this cultural climate, the yellow man decided he would no longer give way to locals walking in the opposite direction on the street. Expecting him to stand aside, they would charge forth and have to dodge him at the last second.

He often wondered what his father would have done in the same situation.

The yellow man's father had also been an actor, although, career-wise, he had not done as well as his son. He had been a disciple of Stanislavski's system of method acting and his tendency towards complex portrayals of the Human Condition had prevented him from succeeding as a type-cast, one-dimensional actor.

In fact, he had been fired from his only proper film role for refusing to take off a New York Yankees baseball cap for a scene. According to him, the cap signified not only the character's childhood fondness for watching the Yankees with his father but also the ultimately fraught nature of that father–son relationship, which had been a key factor in pushing the character to the breaking point he was reaching in the scene.

You're just a guy carrying in a briefcase of cash so the white guy can check it out, the director had said. *You put down the briefcase, stick a knife in the white guy, laugh maniacally. No need for a backstory. You're yellow. You're evil. That's it.*

The yellow man's father became a drunk. He gave up acting and took a job with an office-cleaning company. Every night at dinner, he told his son war stories about losing yellow roles to white men, including one career-making part to Mickey Rooney. Although there was never any proof that it had happened, he always said it was the beginning of the end, losing that part to Mickey.

Such a failure, he once shouted after recounting that story. He threw a bottle of vodka against the wall. *Can't even act my own race.*

Why didn't you just take off the hat for that first movie? his son asked.

You're right. He grabbed his son by the shirt and breathed into his face. *Never aspire to be more than a token yellow. That's how you stay out of trouble. You hear me? One-dimensionality will save your life.*

One day he took off his Yankees cap and left it on the kitchen table with the brim facing his favourite chair. Then he walked to a cliff on the edge of the island and stepped off it into the three-dimensional air, as if the cliff were a flight of stairs and he had failed to notice that there were no more steps.

★

Soon after the yellow man had resolved to stop giving way, he and the yellow woman were leaving a McDonald's on George Street, opposite the cinema from which they had first emerged. The two had become friends, having met through an association for refugees from 3D cinema.

They were sharing a box of fries and heading towards the station when a blond man, neglecting to pay attention to where he was going, walked straight into the yellow man.

Angered by the yellow man's aggression, the blond proposed a fight.

The yellow man refused. Having only ever been a one-dimensional ninja on screen, he knew much less about ninjutsu than about Fellini – an imbalance of knowledge suitable for panel discussions but not for street fights.

Yellow cunt, said the blond man. *Where are your kung fu buddies?*

The blond man king-hit the yellow man. Golden fries – in slow motion – flew into the air and scattered all over the bitumen. The skull of the yellow man split against the kerb.

The blond man spat on the yellow man's face and disappeared.

The yellow man's last thoughts, as his eyes turned to glass, were of a man stepping off the edge of the island, and of a baseball cap abandoned on a kitchen table.

The yellow woman batted away the arms of sympathetic passers-by. She scrabbled about collecting the fries strewn around the yellow man's body, shoving them back into their red cardboard box. She placed the box back into her friend's hands and closed his fingers around it.

She looked up and saw a crowd staring.

Ni hao, she screamed. *Konnichiwa.*

No one replied.

She sat on the kerb and cried. A few people perched next to her and rested their hands on her shoulders. Others tried to revive the yellow man, to no avail. Most, however, continued to stare.

Look at how I've swamped your country, she shouted at them. *I've been selling all your secrets to the yellow people. Your secrets of unreliable public transport and circus-like government. I will kowtow at your restaurant table, lead your men into sin and poison your babies with my cheap synthetic milk and my peasant ways.*

Listen hard to what I'm saying, she said, *because this is the amazing thing I do with my tongue.*

★

For years afterwards, many locals remarked to each other – in the privacy of their own homes and on talkback radio – that the aggressor in the incident had been the yellow man, and that they were deeply concerned by the oversensitive and inflammatory nature of the woman's remarks, by the weak and hysterical character of her emotional display, and by her ingratitude to a nation that had so generously accommodated her, even though she was a member of such a cruel, meek, blank-faced race.

Two

*'As we count up from one, three is the first most interesting
number.'*

– Michael Cunningham

Nothing is known of Ralph's childhood except that he
once dived between the legs of a monk, trying to see if
there was orange underwear under those orange robes.

The monk, laughing, had scooped the little boy up and
held him to the light to see him better. The bald head of
the ascetic gleamed in the morning sun.

'Always remember,' said the monk, 'the fleeting nature
of life. Your past is dead and your future is yet to come.
There is only this moment.'

He set the boy down and went on his way along Circular
Quay. Ralph watched him shuffle past the blind bagpiper
and past the docking ferry, until he disappeared from view.

'If life is fleeting,' Ralph said to himself, 'then I'll beat it.'

Tucked into bed that night, he drew up a checklist for
his life, which he knew would lead him to certain triumph
in this world.

From that moment on, Ralph was in a very big hurry.

★

When it came time to marry, Ralph advertised for a wife in the local newspaper.

There was one applicant.

She perched on Ralph's couch wearing a brown dress covered in large black numbers. The brown was almost indistinguishable from the black and the black almost indistinguishable from the brown. Ralph thought it the ugliest colour combination known to man.

'My name is Lola,' said the girl. 'I'm nineteen.'

'A good vintage,' said Ralph, who wanted to demonstrate his sophistication through viticultural terminology. 'What sort of things do you like?'

'I like chess and dresses,' said Lola, although she had neither a strategic nor a stylish bone in her body.

'I like sports cars that are British racing green,' said Ralph. 'Any colour that races is a good colour.'

'I'm flexible,' said Lola. 'I could like fast cars that are racing green.'

Ralph supposed Lola was physically flexible too, which could make a few items on his checklist quite enjoyable.

'You'll do,' said Ralph.

At the registry, Lola wore a chequered dress. Kings, queens, rooks, bishops, knights and pawns floated on it, tilted at various angles.

Ralph wore his work suit and white sneakers. He always wore sneakers, even to bed.

He had been plagued, for as long as he could remember, with a recurring nightmare in which he was being chased by faceless men. The dream never left him, even in marriage.

He would toss and turn, kicking Lola in the calves while flying over back fences, swinging around Hills hoists and hurdling through low, open windows during the night as sirens wailed and helicopters swung overhead, their search-lights flashing to and fro over garden gnomes and glassy swimming pools.

The sneakers comforted Ralph. If anything went bump in the night, he knew he had good getaway shoes.

★

Ralph and Lola produced twins. The family multiplication happened in the blink of an eye, as if two amoebae had each split in half in an instant.

'Let's call them Maude and Claude,' said Lola, leaning on the kitchen bench with her instant twins strapped to her stomach. She was flicking through a paperback, *Timeless Names for Bouncing Bubs*. 'Maude means "Mighty in Battle". She'd be good at chess.'

'What does Claude mean?'

'"Disabled",' said Lola. 'But I would welcome a disabled child.'

Ralph crossed his arms. 'How about One and Two, for easy reference?'

'I'm flexible,' said Lola as she looked up the names Oanh and Tu, thinking she'd quite like names of ethnic origins.

The relevant item on Ralph's checklist did not say *Children* but *Super Children*.

When Two, much too long after One, took his first steps, Ralph was on the phone.

'What do you take me for? I'm not the sort to bargain for quality. No, I wanted the EBITDA for— Hang on a minute, will you? Yep. Lola? Lola! Why isn't this kid running yet? Is he retarded?'

Two's legs, weak from newness, gave way underneath him. He sat on his nappy with a thud.

Two looked up at Ralph with his very first look of anxiety, blue eyes so big they threatened to take over his face. The look of anxiety had two causes:

1. the inkling that he might never be able to move as fast as his father would like; and
2. the uncomfortable sensation of fresh poop pasted to his bum.

Ralph taught One and Two many things, including how to read a newspaper from cover to cover by the age of three. By their fourth year, they had mastered integration (of the mathematical, rather than racial, kind). By seven, they were mock trading on the stock exchange.

'Buy, buy, buy!' shouted One on the phone to her stockbroker, banging her fist on a plastic blue play table.

'Sell, sell, sell!' shouted Two, knocking over a matching chair in chubby haste.

Yet despite everything Ralph had taught the twins, Two continued to exhibit a clear lack of discipline and self-direction.

Ralph caught him floating in the pool one sunny day, staring up at the overhanging branches of the jacaranda tree and smiling blankly.

His fingers were outstretched, their tips brushing against the purple flowers that floated, delicate and soggy, in the water.

Drifting next to Two was an equally long inflatable banana. It had a blank smile to match.

Ralph became acutely concerned about all that was not going on in that child's brain.

'What are you doing?' Ralph asked.

Two kept floating.

Ralph walked over and stood in Two's sunlight.

Two splashed to attention.

'What are you doing?' Ralph repeated.

'Improving my backstroke?' ventured Two.

What he was really doing was seeing dinosaurs in the clouds and pretending a giant inflatable fruit salad was bobbing around him in the water.

He was also imagining himself as an alien being, his tentacles unrolling over the cobbled edges of the pool, then over the pool gates, creeping through the back door of the house, then through the front door, over the camellias in the front garden, across the main road of the suburb, through the nation's capital, and extending over the oceans to every city in the world, consuming the entire planet.

★

Ralph blew his whistle. He was standing on the side of the local pool, an open-air saltwater monstrosity that looked out over a dark winter sea.

'Freestyle!' he yelled.

Two glanced up in the vague direction of his father. He couldn't see well. He needed his glasses. Treading water, he began to reply, only to be lapped by One. He went under. He coughed and spluttered and cried in the wake of her flutter kicks. He was swallowing salt water and weeping salt water. He had become his own saltwater system.

Two was convinced he was well on the sodden path to death. He ducked under the lane divider and made like a drowning cat towards the blurry feet of his father.

'What do you think you're doing?' said Ralph. 'Finish the lap! And no breaststroke this time. I want freestyle.'

Two rested his forearms on the side of the pool and looked up at Ralph through the fog of his goggles. Water sat unwelcome at the bottom of the eyecups, like two tilting horizons.

'Can I,' Two pleaded, 'use a kickboard?'

Three lanes across the water, students in a swim squad had availed themselves of kickboards, floaties and flippers. This wrapping of children in flotation devices, Ralph thought, would not produce robust individuals with the tenacity to survive in a cutthroat world. Mollycoddling children in this manner was simply not the way of the Ralph Method.

Two realised the futility of his request. Seeing no point in waiting for an answer, he pushed off the wall, wrestled the lane divider and began a sorry freestyle. His kicks were sporadic and he spent most of his time with one arm stretched out in front and his mouth towards the sky, blue-lipped and panting.

Two could never keep up with One, even with a two-lap head start. His sister skimmed the pool like a lithe water insect, barely making a splash.

Two, on the other hand, floundered. His backstroke was consistently diagonal, and whenever the wall of the pool sneaked up behind him, he would yelp. He plodded and stagnated during breaststroke. His butterfly was a dead caterpillar. And each time he saw the bottom of the pool slope radically downwards, he gurgled a prayer to the Virgin Mary – and to Moses, Allah, Ganesha and the Monkey God – for divine protection in the deep end.

In short, swimming, for Two, was like drowning creatively in the cold bath of a giant.

'Out,' said Ralph. 'We're going to work on theory as it pertains to technique, and technique as it pertains to theory.'

Two climbed out of the pool. His legs almost buckled under him. The wind smacked him in the face and carved up his scalp. He wrapped himself in his towel and stood shivering and dripping on the concrete while Ralph demonstrated, with One as his model, the ideal curve of the arm as it enters the water during freestyle.

Two wasn't listening. As he watched One's arm bend and straighten, he noticed how skinny his own arms were in comparison to hers. He wondered if this would become the source of a crippling self-esteem issue in his adolescence and early adulthood.

Once he had stopped thinking about arms, he became mesmerised by the grotesque shapes his father's mouth was forming and by a tiny ball of spittle that was rolling around, untamed, on his father's bottom lip.

Something felt wrong in his stomach.

'I feel sick,' said Two, interrupting Ralph's explanation of the efficiency of the flutter kick.

'No, you don't,' breathed Ralph, partly through the whistle still in his mouth.

'I really do, Ralph,' said Two. Ralph had instructed his twins to address him by his first name for two reasons: firstly, because he believed parenthood to be a type of benevolently dictatorial friendship; and, secondly, because he hoped to avoid situations in crowds where other men might respond to a call for 'Dad' and obscure the direct line of communication between him and his offspring.

'Fine,' said Ralph. 'Be sick. But don't come running to me when you're the only grown fucker on this great fucking island continent who can't fucking swim.'

Two, retching here and there on the way to the car, pulled his glasses out of his terry towelling beach bag. He pushed them onto his face. The first clear thing he saw was Ralph walking at double his speed and never once looking back.

One slowed a little to keep pace with Two. He concentrated on the ground and pretended she wasn't there. He just knew she had that look of pity in her eyes – the same look she gave him when they discovered the body of last year's budgerigar at the bottom of its cage, having met death in the night among newspaper and poop and seed shells. One had turned to Two with a look that asked if he was going to cry. They both knew that he had neglected, the day before, to refill the bird's water feeder and that he had also forgotten to take the cage indoors when the sun went down. It was autumn: the day had been hot and the night had been cold. They never knew which temperature the bird had had a fatal issue with. Maybe both.

'What?' Two had demanded of One, as they stood in front of the cage.

'Ralph said you wouldn't take proper care of a bird. And he was right, wasn't he? Now you've killed it!'

'But it wasn't my fault!' Two, of course, knew where the fault lay but it wasn't One's place to say it. With a messy swing of his fist, he knocked the cage off the table. The two of them stood there in silence, looking at the upended prison and the newspaper inside it, which now shrouded the small corpse.

'Two.' One's voice had become gentler. 'You have to be more aware of what's going on around you. Some things just can't be fixed and this is one of them.'

Now, as they walked behind Ralph away from the pool, One put her hand on Two's shoulder, just as she did when they were staring at the tabloid shroud.

Two shrugged her off.

'Go on,' he said, nodding in the direction of their father. 'I don't care.'

★

Ralph liked to pull the checklist out of his pocket once in a while to check his progress. He also enjoyed crosschecking his performance against a number of laminated copies of the list, which he kept on his desk at work, under the bed next to his spare sneakers and inside his VIP locker at the gym. In addition to these copies, Ralph had miniature versions of the list made the size of credit cards. He kept them in his wallet, under his pillow and stuck to the dashboard of his car, right next to a figurine of an orange-robed monk with a jiggling head that a stripper in Chinatown had produced as a midnight surprise from between her legs.

'I once met a monk just like that,' he would say to those who asked about the figurine. But he couldn't exactly remember the rest of the story.

So far, Ralph had crossed off a wife, two children and four houses. He had also established a company that bought and sold companies that bought and sold other companies. Promoted as always being on the bleeding edge, Ralph's company became so successful that no one in the world acquired money quicker than Ralph did. Neither did anyone make the cover of *TIME* more often than he.

Ralph insisted that all of his cover shots be set in exotic seaside locations. He liked to be photographed sitting by the ocean, with an elbow resting on a bar and a thumb and forefinger positioned on his jaw and cheek, framing his face.

Ralph also insisted that he be shown in every photograph holding a Sea Breeze – made without vodka – in one hand. The slice of lime in the Sea Breeze had to be pierced with a blue paper umbrella on an angle that protected the fruit from the damaging effects of the sun.

'Why a mocktail, not a cocktail?' a reporter once asked.

'Booze is for amateurs,' said Ralph. 'Getting blind drunk on money – now that's the path to happiness.'

Ralph always wore a white shirt for his cover shots. He never wore anything but a white shirt because a very pretty stylist with good legs had once said that no, she didn't want to have a drink with him but yes, a white shirt would bring out his blue eyes. After that day, Ralph never deviated from white, even in daily life. In fact, he discarded his entire shirt collection, replacing it with fourteen identical white shirts that he wore on a fortnightly cycle.

Ralph was also of the opinion that the intense blue of his eyes was further enhanced in each cover shot by his oceanic surroundings.

'Blue eyes and a white shirt by a blue sea,' Ralph would say to the photographer. 'It's a win-win combo.'

It was always the same photographer who took Ralph's cover shots. To her dismay, she couldn't seem to escape Ralph-related assignments. She would snap away as Ralph talked about his win-win combo, thinking it was surely a win-win-win combo but reminding herself that nowhere in the brief was she required to concern herself with the correction of fools.

Ralph made it to the cover of *TIME* at least once a year. He took to having each new cover framed in platinum and hung alongside the others in a row that stretched down the hallway of his favourite house.

To commemorate each new addition to the collection, he would put the family dog on a leash and sprint the winding streets to the top of the cliff in his suburb.

At the peak, with sweat gathering over his top lip and on his temples, Ralph would look out over the ocean and make a strange shrill call and beat his chest.

'Conquered Time yet again,' Ralph would say to the dog, before yanking the leash in the direction of home.

★

Reports sent home from Two's primary school said that, although he was a Gifted and Talented Individual, he Lacked Focus. He was known to talk incessantly about topics unrelated to the curriculum, such as the poetry of Coleridge, whose rhyme about the mariner, one of the reports said, did not need to be written out in full on a poster that was supposed to explain the meaning of Gross Domestic Product.

At home, Two was performing even worse. He spent every spare hour reading books on obscure topics like lotus cultivation in Asia. He was also a great fan of treatises by pop philosophers who pondered the significance of the Melting Moment in the life of the modern individual.

When Ralph asked Two to draw up his own life checklist, Two wrote it in pink crayon on the back of a failed test on complex numbers. His list included making a terrarium, learning how to whistle with his fingers, and putting his hand into the Mouth of Truth without having it bitten off.

'What sort of loser list is this?' asked Ralph.

Two had brought a plate of Melting Moments as a visual aid to enhance communication with Ralph during their checklist meeting, which he knew would be difficult territory. Earlier that day, Two had snooped around One's desk while she was out swimming laps and had discovered that her list was typed, printed and laminated, just like Ralph's, and included stellar items such as *World Record for Distance Swum from Australia.*

So when Ralph opened with that loser question, Two was well prepared to defend himself. He took a deep breath and began what he had rehearsed.

'The reason I brought these biscuits was to show you that—'

But Ralph had already inhaled them all, like a monster out of a picture book.

'Yum yum,' went Ralph. 'Munch, munch.'

★

'This girl's a magician.' Ralph was leaning over his PA's desk, watching her type. He winked. 'I do love magic.'

Two wondered what sort of magic Ralph was talking about. Ralph had brought Two to company headquarters for the day to show him what he could become if he just had some focus. Two had been trailing after Ralph all morning, reading a book that had a black and white photo on the cover, of an old man with a white beard and round glasses, dressed in a woollen suit.

'This is Two,' Ralph said, introducing him to the senior managers, the managers, the graduates, the secretaries, the interns, the computers and the air-purifying pot plants. A pair of secretaries squealed over Two and pinched his cheeks, their fingers and thumbs straightened like tweezers so that their aggressive manicures wouldn't leave marks on his virgin skin.

'Hiya, Two,' they said in unison.

'Hi,' said Two, looking up from Freud and wondering how any field of endeavour could involve so many boring-looking people in such boring-looking clothes. He wondered why they pretended to be so boring when, most likely, they were all making sweet magic in the stationery room after hours, ties flung over shoulders, manicures up against the frosted glass of the door, with the cupboards and the notepads and the highlighters and paperclips and staplers and coloured Post-its and packets of alphabetical tab dividers all jolting in time with every thrust.

After work, Ralph stood in the underground car park flicking through emails on his BlackBerry while his newest employee packed folders into the boot of Ralph's car.

The new addition to Ralph's team was in his first week of induction. His official function at the company was to be available full-time as Ralph's stand-in whenever Ralph was out of the office. Ralph liked to call this employee his 'personal avatar'. The avatar was a handsome, unintimidating, out-of-work actor who was to be referred to as Razza in order to cultivate the impression that there was a more approachable, and indeed even buddy-like, dimension to Ralph's personality, particularly when he was not present.

Although it was technically inappropriate for them to be in the same room at the same time, Ralph was finding Razza to be of additional use as a companion in the running of unavoidable errands and in the parenting of unavoidable children.

While gazing at his new hire with a feeling of self-admiration, Ralph noticed Two shuffling around the car park, still engrossed in his book. The boy looked up and saw the disappointment in his father's eyes.

'Reading and walking,' said Two. 'I'm multitasking.'

'God Almighty,' said Ralph. 'Put that book down and give Razza a hand.'

'Ralph?' Two peered at his father through chipped tortoiseshell glasses that occupied half his face. Ralph thought the glasses were ridiculous. Two had insisted on having the biggest lenses available so he could roll his eyes right around his field of vision and be able to see everything in focus. Ralph and the optometrist had suggested that Two wear sleeker glasses like the kids at school but Two wouldn't have anything to do with a short-sighted idea like that.

'Ralph!' Two said again.

'What?'

'Would you say that your first sexual impulse was towards your mother?'

'Get in the car,' said Ralph.

Ralph's car was a Lotus. Two wondered why it was called a Lotus if it didn't look or smell or sound like a flower, or sit in a pond all day.

The Lotus was British racing green. It had two yellow stripes on top, running from front to back. Two thought it looked like a sled had run over a flock of canaries in a forest clearing.

'Why do you have a racing car?' asked Two. 'There aren't any autobahns around.'

Ralph huffed and sighed.

'I have a Roadster, Two, because I want to know I can outdrive a cyclone if the occasion ever calls for it. We are cyclone-ready. We are a cyclone-ready family.'

'But cyclones never come here,' said Two. 'If we lived in Kansas, on the other hand, like Dorothy—'

'We are not in Kansas. We are not Dorothy. We are cyclone-ready.' Ralph was quite taken with how his succinct, on-message delivery of these facts incorporated the repetition of the inclusive 'we'. He realised that this approach might also prove useful in his next company-wide video message, during which he would unveil the exceptionally inclusive new redundancy program.

'The other reason we have a fast car,' said Ralph, 'is that life is about position. The number of cars you have in your rear-vision mirror is the number of suckers you are beating at any given moment in the race.'

To demonstrate his point, he revved the engine and wove in and out of traffic with just one hand on the steering wheel, overtaking three cars at a time, even on the bends.

Two gripped the sides of his seat and vomited his lunch into his lap.

I am pondering, wrote Two in his diary that night, *how these dysfunctional father–son dynamics will affect my psychological wellbeing later in life*. He tapped the end of his pencil against his bottom lip and contemplated methods for minimising the damage.

After an intense brainstorm, involving an entire packet of connector pens, Two concluded that the key to improving his relationship with his father must be to engineer some sort of sentimental connection over a common interest, or, at the very least, an interest of Ralph's that Two could pretend to share.

Pleased with his progress, the budding therapist closed his diary, slid it under his pillow and had a nightmare that

Ralph was teaching him to drive. Two was cross-eyed the whole time. He couldn't see straight through the bending, swerving, groaning traffic.

★

'Smell it,' said Two, fanning a deck of cards under Ralph's nose. 'Isn't it good?'

Ralph jerked his head away. He was on the couch, reviewing on his laptop a spreadsheet Razza had prepared, which forecasted the future growth of a company belonging to an eccentric mining magnate who was notorious for his obsession with steamrollers. Ralph had been toying with the idea of getting into the mining game and Razza, hoping to impress his new boss, had created the spreadsheet off his own bat. Apparently the out-of-work actor was not just handsome but also a commerce graduate with a credit average.

'Take any card,' said Two. 'Any card at all.'

Ralph pulled one from the proffered spread, with his eyes still fixed on the screen.

'Which one is it?'

'What?' said Ralph, trying to delete a row.

'Which card do you have?'

Ralph flipped it over.

'Jack of hearts.'

Two grinned. 'And what was the card you got before?'

'Honestly, Two, I don't remember.'

'Come on. *The jack of hearts!* The exact same card!'

'Fuck.' Ralph had accidentally changed a formula that had altered all the numbers in column C. 'Where's that fucking PA when you need her? Oh, that's right. Off in the Bahamas personally assisting some wanker in bed. Fuck. Fuck. Fuck.'

'See, Ralph?' said Two, getting the feeling that Ralph's attention was not entirely on the magical proceedings at hand. 'Wasn't that amazing?'

'I don't have time for idiot tricks,' said Ralph, hunched over the laptop and clicking madly. 'Tell you what would be magic? If you fixed this fucking spreadsheet.'

Two sat on the verandah. He looked at the two-headed jack of hearts and that blow-dried golden hair. The jack, drawn in profile, was looking across at a red heart. He had a blue eyebrow, a blue nose, a blue moustache and a blue mouth. His sad blue eye had a blue line under it. He looked tired.

Two rotated the card so he could see the jack's opposite head, which still looked sad. He had the same eternal expression, whichever way you looked at him.

Two took a black texta from his shirt pocket. He wrote *RALPH IS A FUCK FUCK FUCK* over the two faces. Then he pushed the card into the soil of a potted geranium so that one sad head remained upright, staring at the front door, and the other was buried, suffocating in the dirt under the weight of its better half.

★

There was a new boy in Year Five called Stefan.

'Not my real name,' he said as he shook Two's hand. They were sitting on a low brick wall at recess watching the other kids running around and squealing. 'I'm in a witness protection program.'

'Oh,' said Two.

Stefan pushed up his sleeve, exposing a freckled arm. 'A gang did this to me. Homemade tattoo gun.'

The tattoo in question looked a lot like a scribble. It also looked a lot like it had been done in the last five minutes with a blue ballpoint Kilometrico pen.

'So what are you in here for?' asked Stefan.

'Eternity,' said Two.

'You're smart. What does your dad do?'

'Ralph buys and sells companies that buy and sell companies.'

'Impressive.'

'Brutal,' said Two. 'But, as Ralph always says: "Life is brutal, why fight it?"'

'I don't know anyone who says that,' said Stefan.

'What does your dad do?'

'I'm an orphan.' Stefan lifted part of a scab on his knee and examined the raw pink underneath.

'I'm sorry,' said Two.

'My parents fell to their deaths in a freak hang-gliding accident on their ninth anniversary off the coast of Rio de Janeiro.'

Two's eyes had already started to water.

'Why are you crying?' asked Stefan.

'I can't help it,' said Two. 'Ralph says I'm a bleeding heart.'

Two cried and cried, thinking of the constant haemorrhaging of his heart, the inherent unfairness of life, the blue sky, the wayward gliding and the freaky but fatal coast of Rio.

That night, over dinner, One said to Two:

'That new kid, Stefan. His dad does the same thing as Ralph. Buys and sells companies that buy and sell companies.'

'Who told you that?'

'He did.'

'Same as Ralph, eh?'

Two narrowed his red eyes and stemmed the bleeding inside his chest.

The next morning, Two lined up behind Stefan for rollcall on the bitumen netball court.

'Hey,' said Two. 'Heard you resurrected your dad.'

'What?'

'Look,' said Two, 'I don't know what trauma came to pass in your early childhood but you're hired.'

The final agreement was five marbles a day.

'The big clear ones with the swirls inside,' said Stefan. 'Or it's no deal.'

'What do you take me for?' said Two. 'I'm not the sort to bargain for quality.'

It was only when they were halfway to Narrabeen on a father–son daytrip strongly recommended by the school counsellor that Ralph noticed a duplicate boy in his rear-view mirror. He pulled the Lotus over to the side of the road.

'Who's this?'

'My avatar,' said Two. 'In training.'

Two II, formerly known as Stefan, grinned at Ralph, thinking only of his imminent wealth: five marbles for the day and two marbles' holiday loading.

'Gnarly,' said Razza, in keeping with the day's beach theme.

Ralph made a mental note on his mental clipboard to address this inappropriate use of language in Razza's annual performance review.

Razza was assigned the task of teaching Two how to fish.

'Don't worry, I'm right behind you,' he said, as Two stepped onto the narrow concrete wall leading out to the rock shelf.

Once they were there, Razza produced a lunchbox full of live worms.

'Let's teach you how to hook one of these.'

The thought of even touching a worm turned Razza's stomach but he put on his best fishing face, took one of the squirming things and layered it onto the hook. Two watched the creature twist and turn – a length of straining, suffering muscle.

'I feel sick,' said Two, interrupting Razza's improvised explanation of the efficiency of using live, rather than plastic, bait.

'Shit,' said Razza.

'I really, really feel sick,' said Two.

'Here.' Razza handed him the yellow bucket meant for the fish.

Two vomited into it. But the acid taste in his mouth didn't bother him because Razza's hand was on his elbow and Razza's voice was saying softly in his ear:

'Hey, little fella. Let's get you cleaned up.'

Later, the two went for a gentle walk along the beach. They picked their way through dead bluebottles to the edge of the water and stood staring out at the horizon.

Each time the waves drew back, Two felt the sand pulling away from under his feet. He half-panicked that the sand would suck him right under the ocean and drown him. But he knew it wasn't going to happen that day because Razza was there.

'I like you, Razza,' said Two. 'More than Ralph.'

'Gnarly,' said Razza, feeling that less was more in playing this beach scene.

Having taken over operations at the rock shelf, Ralph was reeling in a jewfish.

'I'll deal with it,' said Two II. He unhooked it, took it by the tail and bashed its brains out on the rocks.

'Unorthodox,' said Ralph, 'but shows initiative.'

Two II shrugged. 'Life is brutal. Why fight it?'

Ralph ruffled the hair of the duplicate child and decided that this was a boy he had the right skill set to raise. Two II smiled up at him.

'Your father must be proud of you,' said Ralph.

'My real dad's a drug lord,' said Two II. 'He'd give me up for a bag of crack.'

'People should have licences to have children,' Ralph said and cast his line back into the sea.

The sun was setting. Two was crouched in the sand with his camera, looking for a nice way to frame the view, when he noticed Razza and Two II within shot.

They were far off in the distance, walking down the beach. Razza was ruffling Two II's hair and resting his hand on the boy's shoulder – a perfect moment between avatar father and avatar son.

Two let the camera drop around his neck. He ruffled his own hair and wondered why it wasn't innately lovable. After all, it was the same honey colour as Stefan's and dropped over his eyes in the same way. Yet it wasn't loved, thought Two, not even by a faux father who'd been hired to faux love him.

Ralph was standing next to Two, seeing what he was seeing, both of them unable to look away from the pair.

'I want to go home to Lola,' said Two, after a while.

'We're going,' said Ralph. 'Don't you worry about that.'

Two was no fool. He knew in his gut that if Razza's heart belonged to another, he would have to take swift and decisive action.

That night, in the semi-darkness of Two II's parents' front lawn, with the verandah light illuminating the boys' honey-coloured hair, Two made his smirking avatar redundant, citing budget cuts due to slowing growth in the marble economy.

★

As soon as Stefan's very alive, very law-abiding parents had retracted all allegations of kidnapping against Ralph, and life had returned to normal, Ralph decided it would be a good time to take stock of all he had acquired.

Why is everything so old? he thought as he inspected his favourite house. The carpet had worn thin and mould was creeping down the walls. He ran a finger along the sideboard, leaving a mahogany-coloured streak in the thick layer of dust.

Then he noticed that, sometime in the last ten years of their marriage, Lola had turned into a table lamp. She wasn't even an attractive one – brown with black numbers and frayed at the edges.

Ralph realised things had progressed in a direction with which he was not entirely comfortable.

'I can't stay the husband of an item of furniture,' he said to the lamp.

The lamp flickered as if to say: 'I'm flexible.'

A tear rolled down its shade.

'Be careful,' Ralph said, as he put the lamp out on the street for the council's next bulk waste collection. 'No need to get all teary and electrocute yourself on account of me.'

★

In the spirit of renewal, Ralph bought another house for himself and his numbered offspring. The house was big and white, full of sharp edges and cold marble floors. Ralph hired men dressed in green jumpsuits and green caps to remove the grass and lay down artificial lawn, in order to produce, instantly and permanently, the effect of a well-tended garden.

One night at the dinner table, Ralph rubbed his hands together.

'Do I have a surprise for you.' He produced a stack of pages that his PA had prepared. 'The checklist says I have to see the world and you're coming with me. Our whole holiday is set out in this spreadsheet.'

When laid out end to end, the pages of the spreadsheet stretched from the front to the back door and back again.

'We're going to cover every single city in existence,' said Ralph to his offspring, as he walked them through it, 'at a minimum rate of one a day.'

One's eyes shone as if she had just seen a tower of chocolate sprout from the ground. She knelt next to the spreadsheet for a closer look.

'As you can see,' said Ralph, 'our movements for each day have been broken down into five-minute blocks.'

Two mooched back to the dining room, sat in his allocated spot and stared into his chicken soup. His only comfort in the world at that moment was the warmth his palms felt against the sides of his bowl.

'Be careful,' Ralph said. 'No need to get all teary, even if it is with joy.'

There were documented holiday policies and procedures to ensure that One and Two kept up the appropriate pace.

They were on a minibus leaving the Leaning Tower of Pisa when Ralph said: 'This calls for Protocol Number Three.'

He handed Two a video camera.

'Sorry, Ralph, what's Number Three?'

'I quizzed you at Heathrow.'

'I know,' said Two. 'I'm really sorry.'

'Just point this out the window and stop recording when I say so.'

Two pushed the lens up against the glass and pressed the red button. His arm ached all the way through the blur of Florence and Rome, and a red circle formed around his right eye from the pressure of the suction-cupped view-finder. When the minibus drew up to St Peter's Basilica, its last stop for the day, Ralph looked up from his BlackBerry and asked why the hell Two was still recording.

While the trio caught an orchestral performance in Vienna, Ralph made the children watch a *Highlights of Italy* package on his BlackBerry. The video had been edited from Two's Protocol Three footage by Ralph's PA back at company headquarters.

'Goes pretty well with this music,' said Ralph, rather surprised. The patrons behind them stared in fury at the back of his head.

As Ralph and the twins sipped mocktails in Vanuatu, they began writing postcards home. These particular postcards had been picked up in Cambodia, so Ralph insisted they all be backdated to the day the family sped through that country on the back of a ute.

Hello from Siem Reap, wrote Ralph to the CEO of a company he had just bought. He wrote so quickly that none of his loops joined up. His As and Os all looked like Us, while his Es looked like Ls and his Ls looked like Es. In Two's eyes, the message appeared to say *Hleeu frum Silm*

Rlup as if the letters were floating around a bubbling pot of turtle soup.

That night, One whispered to Two that she thought Ralph's handwriting looked like a pigeon had had a case of bad worms, shat all over the page and then hopped through its own poopsie lala. They giggled and snorted together, both sandwiched flat on their backs between the hotel's starched white sheets.

But Ralph couldn't care less about his handwriting. He called this Efficient Personal Time Management, or EPTM, which he saw as a cornerstone of the company that bought and sold other companies. Ralph's rationale was that the less time he spent writing these holiday greetings, the more time the recipients would be forced to spend attempting to read them. He felt this distribution of intellectual labour to be appropriate.

The photo featured on the postcard from Silm Rlup showed an ancient tree spreading its roots over an ancient building. Ralph didn't like how old the whole scene looked. He made a mental note to email the concierge who had given him the postcards and have him rethink the hotel's postcard acquisition strategy, on the basis that a country should always promote itself as being on the bleeding edge.

While finishing his postcard, Ralph texted an employee to acquire another company he wanted.

Have it done by yesterday. Thx. R, said the text.

In the middle of both writing and texting, Ralph elbowed Two. 'The Four-In-One Experience,' he said. 'Having mocktails in Vanuatu while sending postcards from Siem Reap while acquiring MetCo from StetCo while spending quality time with the kids. This is the beauty of multitasking.'

'I don't like multitasking,' said Two and burst into tears.

'You read and walk at the same time. That's multitasking.'

'Can we stop?' asked Two. 'I'm tired.'

'We can't have anyone holding up this holiday,' said Ralph. 'There's no room for delay.'

'I cannot proceed,' said Two. 'There is a high risk I will begin to exhibit symptoms of a panic attack if I am forced to continue with this ill-advised mode of action.'

Ralph shrugged. 'Suit yourself.'

He stuffed a return plane ticket into Two's shirt pocket and sent him and his psychological baggage straight back to their great island nation.

'How about you?' Ralph asked One, once he had dispatched his recalcitrant second child.

'I can keep up,' One said with a brave face. She wiped her clammy hands on her dress, the fabric of which was printed with maps of major European cities.

But One knew her own stride was only half her father's. Inevitably, during a second dash around the globe to cover cities they had accidentally missed, Ralph outran One, leaving her waiting by Manneken Pis, that famous statue in Brussels of a small boy taking a public slash.

*

Back from holidays, Ralph put out a second advertisement.

The consequent upgrade wife, who had no associated children, was called Silvia. At the interview, Ralph and Silvia ran their checklists by an algorithm designed to calculate their relationship potential. The algorithm, which took into account 216 dimensions of compatibility such as calf length and hair growth rate, determined that Ralph and Silvia were ninety-seven per cent compatible. Unsatisfied with this result yet unwilling to spend any more time searching for a suitable candidate, Ralph asked Silvia to be his bride and Silvia, experiencing a ninety-seven per cent compatible emotional meltdown, said yes.

Silvia was not one bit like Lola. She was the sort who would never turn into a lamp. 'Only the Best for Silvia' was her motto. She liked floral rather than chess dresses, resembling more a supermarket bouquet than a board game. She invariably wore her hair in a lacquered French roll.

Said Silvia to her eleven girlfriends between sips of Lady Grey in the tearoom of a swish hotel:

'He's quick to lose people. But I'll change him.'

The girlfriends arched their collective eyebrows and brought their porcelain cups to their pursed lips, in the manner of those who must stoically and silently look on as their loved ones make foolish life decisions.

'Ninety-seven per cent made for each other,' said one, snapping the lips of her purse together as they watched Silvia flounce off in the cloth bouquet of the day.

At the wedding, as the guests toasted the lucky couple in a field of sunflowers, Ralph lifted Silvia's veil for a kiss. Both veil and dress had been printed with photorealistic, life-sized sunflowers, a design that inadvertently caused Silvia to blend seamlessly with her surroundings. The guests had been unaware of her presence until the moment the celebrant asked that they stand for the bride.

Upon lifting Silvia's veil, all Ralph could see was a hovering head with painted red lips opening towards him in slow motion. He suffered. His mind screamed that he was in the middle of a mistake and he felt sick in his stomach, like the few times in his life when he had tripped and realised, mid-fall, that it was too late for him to avert a brutal landing.

In the end, the only course of action Ralph could take to make those lips go away was to give them a peck.

Overjoyed, Silvia beamed at her eleven bridesmaids of the pursed lips and lipped purses, who were also swathed in photorealistic, life-sized sunflower gowns. Ralph couldn't bring himself to look at the dozen floating heads and their painted smiles. He stared at his trusty sneakers and bounced up and down on the balls of his feet, as if he were a lunchtime runner in the CBD, sporting a company T-shirt, short shorts and hairy legs, and waiting at a traffic light for the little man to go green.

At the reception, Ralph watched Silvia giggle as her bridesmaids arranged her train, helping to prepare her for the throwing of the bouquet. He turned to his PA.

'Put the divorce in my calendar for a year from now.'

'Pardon?' said the PA, who was hitching up her dress to jostle for a good bouquet-catching position on the dance floor.

'Look at her fussing over those flowers,' said Ralph. 'This one's too slow for my liking.'

The PA wondered why Ralph had a problem with Silvia's speed when really what he should have been concerned about were the myriad ways in which Silvia's face looked like that of a powdered horse.

As Ralph watched the sunflowers arc through the air, he resolved that one day he would find and marry a girl from a wealthy racing family, who understood the need for speed – someone unlike this woman with the slow red lips, who looked like a thoroughbred but was sure to usher him to a premature death-by-boredom in between sips of Lady Grey in the tearooms of endless swish hotels.

★

After Silvia, there was a procession of women. Ralph chose them as young as they legally came until it dawned on him that their youth was making him feel older, not younger.

They would look at him out of the corners of their eyes, toss their hair to one side and smooth out the laps of their assorted dresses, asking:

'Bill Gates? Is he a comedian?' and, 'Which Korea is evil, East or West?'

Ralph was strolling one day down his hallway of cover shots when he stopped suddenly. He stepped over to one of the more recent pictures and put his face so close to it that his real nose touched his magazine nose. Staring deep into his own eyes, Ralph realised that the photographs in these platinum frames had been recording not just his career successes from year to year but also his physical deterioration.

He hurried back to the very first picture and walked again down the hallway, scrutinising each photograph. He saw for the first time how the two lines on his forehead were settling into position, how the groove between his eyebrows was deepening into a chasm and how the skin on his neck was growing more and more like that of a plucked chicken.

After that day, he refused all cover shots. At least in the world of glossy print, Ralph was preserved at a trim, blue-eyed fifty.

★

Old age, when it truly arrived, made Ralph spill cups of tea and fall off ladders. It put glue in his eyes and made him smell like old coats. His knuckles swelled and his skin turned to creased leather, marked with inexplicable stains. He played unwilling host to stray white hairs that reached out in curls from his nose and ears. The hair on his head turned to straw. It sat at strange angles and couldn't be brushed flat into an acceptable hairstyle. It rustled in the wind, like bamboo, and dropped off with the autumn breeze in accordance with a schedule to which Ralph had not agreed.

Ralph began to wear a promotional cap from the Whistling Lakes Golf Club, where he was a member.

'I'm getting a thousand a second to wear this,' he declared to anyone who would listen, though the real purpose of the hat was to keep each hair on his head for at least a solid day longer than its use-by date.

To accompany the line, he would mime a golf swing and squint out at the horizon.

'A physical representation of my financial hole-in-one,' he would add for those who stared at him without comprehension.

They were justifiably confused about what the old man was trying to mime. His agility wasn't what it used to be and the swing ended up looking more like a prolonged tai chi move that might be called Painting the Upside Down Boat Rainbow of the Emperor's Blue Mooncake.

Although Ralph's finances were doing brilliantly on his metaphorical golf course, they were, in reality, heading for disaster.

Ralph had once been considered a game-changing entrepreneurial wizard. The business model on which his company was founded had been copied so frantically across the globe that commentators declared there had not been a craze this crazily crazy since the Dutch tulip mania of the 1600s.

Unfortunately, it also turned out that the crazily crazy craze in companies that bought and sold companies that bought and sold companies was unsustainable.

The bubble burst with Ralph inside it, mid-swing.

On the day Ralph's fortune performed a vanishing act in the top stories of every major news outlet, Ralph's latest wife – who had been raised in a greyhound-racing dynasty and had the glint of acquisition in her eye – became distracted by an attractive piece of man meat. In the instant it flashed by, she decided to seize the opportunity and leave this doddering fool behind because if time was fleeting, she would beat it.

★

When it came time for Ralph to move to a nursing home, only Two was left to guide him into the waiting taxi.

Razza was long gone. He'd sat down and calculated,

with a spreadsheet, the future growth of his corporate career, consequently jumping ship before the bursting of Ralph's bubble, and taking up a new gig as an avatar, Bazza, for the mining magnate with the penchant for steamrollers.

As for One, she had long since used the skills she had gained from the Ralph Method to escape across the ocean.

At fifteen, she had practised her getaway by swimming Bass Strait. Ralph had hired a film crew to record the attempt. The waves on the day had been high and treacherous and it looked like One would have to give up.

In a short window of calm across the water, Ralph had used a fishing rod to lower a bottle of liquid breakfast from the boat to his daughter. One trod water and drank from the bottle. She had been daubed in sunscreen and still had streaks of it on her cheeks and chin.

'Drink it all,' shouted Ralph.

'Yes, Ralph,' said One.

When she was done with the breakfast, Ralph lowered a replacement pair of goggles.

'Make sure you get the goggles on right,' shouted Ralph.

'Yes, Ralph,' said One.

'Just ninety-two kilometres to go,' said a commentator who had come as part of the crew hire package. 'Do you think you'll make it?'

'Do you think I'll make it? One day I'm going to swim so far you can't catch me,' said One, and she looked dead straight into the camera.

Ralph twitched.

'It isn't humanly possible to swim from here to another country,' said Ralph as One resumed her freestyle. The camera stayed on him as he concentrated on winding up the fishing line. 'She's delirious from the swim. Delirious from the swim,' he repeated over and over to no one and everyone and himself.

He maintained this conviction until the day she really did jump into the ocean to swim far, far away.

One had left Two a note sticking out of his Freud.

Some things just can't be fixed, it said, *and Ralph is one of them*.

When Two discovered that One had swum away from home, he refused to leave his room for weeks.

His life, he knew, had been ruined by scrawny arms. If he had been stronger and better with a paddle, One might have decided to take him with her.

He had always assumed they would make a break together, in one defining moment when the past would drop cleanly away. But now he was stuck here, alone, on this great fucking island continent, a failed disciple of the Ralph Method.

Two spent all his time watching an old Hollywood farce on repeat. The plot of the film involved a gumshoe who was hot on the trail of an international double agent in a purple cape and waxed moustache. A dashed line on a cartoon map tracked for the audience the movements of the villain from Belize to Cairo to Saint Petersburg to the East Siberian Sea, where the line finally petered out and was replaced with a big white question mark.

And Two, in the darkness of his room, would begin to cry, no longer knowing the whereabouts of that one person who would have put her hand on his shoulder at a time like this.

★

On the day the taxi arrived to take his father to the nursing home, Two was already fifty. Decades before, he had made what Ralph had declared to be The Most Irrational, Economically Humiliating Career Choice Possible For This Historical Moment. He had become a poet.

To pay the rent, he worked six days a week at the country's fastest-growing gym chain. His job was to make phone calls to individuals who had signed up in shopping centres for free gym trials. Sometimes he managed to arrange for them to come in for a personalised introduction to their local branch; other times he was told to shut his face, *you Indian call centre freak.*

Two worked nights on his poetry and had chronic injuries from typing, so that he went around with his wrists permanently in bandages. At first, his colleagues at the gym thought he had been overdoing the wrist curls, but given his demonstrated lack of interest in physical activity, as well as his enduring inability to achieve any of his annual performance targets, they later came to believe that he was such a failure in life that he couldn't even succeed in committing suicide.

Two was visiting Ralph in the nursing home when Ralph asked, as he often did, what had become of Two II.

'Council worker,' said Two. 'They pay him to get chewing gum off the footpath with a putty knife.'

In reality, Stefan had given up lying for marbles and now worked in a glass tower, lying instead for thousand-dollar dress shoes to go with his thousand-dollar suits.

'What have you been up to?' asked Ralph.

'Funny you should ask,' said Two. The reason for his visit was to announce to Ralph that he had had a piece accepted by the arts magazine *Human Waste*. The magazine's point of difference from other underground publications was that it was printed on recycled toilet paper and came in a roll.

Two unwound the magazine to square twenty-three, on which his poem was printed, and showed it to Ralph.

'It's only eighteen words long,' said Ralph.

'Twenty, if you include the title.'

'How much did they pay you for it?'

'A six-pack of blank toilet rolls.'

'So, a third of a roll per word,' said Ralph. 'They got a good deal there.'

'But,' said Two, 'what if this poem is the answer to the meaning of life?'

'Is it?' asked Ralph. 'Is the answer in this line about the difference between spiral and flat pasta?'

Two saw his point. But what they both failed to realise, like all those who miss the secret of the Universe even though it is right under their noses, was that the answer lay in the enjambed line about the extra virgin olive oil.

Ralph, on his own initiative, conducted hourly tests of the nursing home's emergency call system.

'Just confirming response times are on the bleeding edge,' he would explain when staff arrived.

He was on pills to regulate his heartbeat, pills to thin his blood, pills to reduce his cholesterol levels and pills to strengthen his bones. He was on pills to regulate his anxiety, pills to numb his depression and pills to make him sleep. His legs had given way completely, everything sounded to him like he was stuck at the end of a padded tunnel, and he peed every time he sneezed.

Two became acutely concerned about all that was not going on in the old man's brain. Ralph's mind had begun to forget everything at an accelerating rate. In the space of a day, he had lost the ability to read the difference between three and nine o'clock. Once, he had even gone missing from the home and was found outside a chess convention attempting to bully a table lamp into taking him back.

The nursing home's resident psychiatrist was sent to observe Ralph's conversations with inanimate objects. Ralph assumed the psychiatrist was his PA and ordered her to send for Razza to be old and sick in his place, because Ralph didn't have time for all this crap.

Ralph's mind deteriorated to a stage where there was no way he would even be able to pick his nurses out of a line-up, which later became a problem when one really did need to be picked out of a line-up for putting Ralph's Culturally and Linguistically Diverse roommate, Anastasio, in an acid bath.

Two visited every morning. He would retie the shoelaces of Ralph's sneakers, switch on Ralph's hearing aids and whisper in his ear: 'Let's go.'

He would haul Ralph into his wheelchair, spin it around and run him up and down corridors at unnatural, dizzying speeds.

Then they would rest. Two would spoon porridge into Ralph's mouth as they sat outside under a hexagonal pergola, next to a shrivelled woman with crimped hair who was convinced she was inside the command centre of an Unidentified Flying Object and had been sent to beg the alien-Two for mercy on behalf of the human race.

The porridge would dribble down Ralph's chin while Two talked to him about speed. About how fast Freud had come up with his theories, even though they were the work of a lifetime. About how you can only truly appreciate how fast a car is going by watching from the side of the road, rather than having your foot on the pedal.

And every day Ralph gripped the seat of his wheelchair and felt like throwing up, but he managed to force a smile as he waited for this young stranger's little romantic scene to be over. The boy, after all, was wearing bandages on his wrists, and Ralph knew to be careful with suicidal fools.

Ralph couldn't stem the bleeding of his heart but he didn't know why. All he knew was that he had on his getaway shoes but there was nowhere left to run.

★

Ralph was dying.

Two sat on a metal chair next to his bed in the nursing home and on the radio Ella Fitzgerald was singing how she couldn't give him anything but love, baby. Two wasn't sure Ralph could hear her. Ralph's eyes were open and unseeing. An infection was in his brain and there wasn't a pill for it. His head jerked from left to right to left to right all day and all night.

★

Two woke from the warmth of the sun on his eyelids. He shifted in his chair. First he saw the window he forgot to close in the night. Next he saw his father, motionless. He crept up to watch Ralph's chest for movement.

There was nothing.

Two felt like a little boy standing over the cage of a dead bird, knowing that this was a calamity that could not be fixed. He wondered if his father had been too hot in the night from the extra blanket Two had used to tuck him in, or if he had been too cold from the winter chill breathing through the window.

Maybe in the end, he thought, everything is about temperature, not speed. He supposed that, if Ralph had chosen this as his arbitrary philosophy, Two might have been raised in a climate-controlled chamber, or even warm in an oven like a loaf of bread.

He laughed.

A nurse who had run in to attend to Ralph was horrified that a son could be sniggering at a time like this.

Two didn't notice her in the room.

Sand was drawing away from under his feet, sucking him below to the seabed and into the heavy folds of the ocean. The weight of all that water was sitting on his chest and in his throat.

Somewhere up above, nurses and doctors and more

nurses were trying to talk to him. He couldn't hear any of it. There was too much water between them.

The water scared him. He was the little boy again with the weak arms, crying to Mary and Moses and Allah and Ganesha and the Monkey God to take it all away, to drink up the sea because he couldn't breathe.

Then he saw Ralph lying next to him, still shrouded in blankets.

Two stopped struggling.

He rested his hand on Ralph's shoulder and sat by him for the longest time until there was no water anymore, just the two of them and the open window and the winter air.

The more Two watched, the more he realised that this dead body had little in common with his father. Whatever made Ralph Ralph was no longer in this room.

When the bed had been cleared and Two was sitting wordless under the pergola next to the UFO Ambassador, a nurse put an envelope in his hand.

'It was under his pillow,' she said.

'Ah,' said Two. 'The list.'

★

Two is standing on the cliff where Ralph used to beat his chest.

He has come here to cross off Ralph's final, unwritten item and to burn the list, leaving its ashes to vanish with the wind.

But when he opens the envelope, the list isn't there.

In its place is the defaced jack of hearts.

Two holds the card to the light to see it better. Then he sets the jack down against a rock, so that its one blue eye can look out over the ocean.

He steps back and regards it with a smile.

A win-win combo, he thinks.

Following the jack's gaze across the water, Two squints at the rising sun.

He puts his fingers to his mouth and gives a sharp whistle that he imagines One can hear somewhere out there.

Once he is done, Two takes himself to the local pool to swallow salt water and weep salt water and be his own saltwater system.

Then he floats on his back and spreads his alien tentacles over the world.

Slow Death in Cat Cafe

A cat cafe in Strathfield, in the state of New South Wales, is seceding from the Australian nation.

The owner of the cafe, a balding Chinese man, declares his intention to secede over a loudspeaker while I'm sitting on the blond wood floor of his establishment eating a slice of Meow Meow Mud Cake.

The man wants to transform the cat cafe, called Cat Cafe, into a micronation called the Republic of Cat Cafe.

He has a list of justifications, which he reads out.

First, he objects to local council's obsession with hygiene, in particular its draconian ban on the presence of cats in areas where food is served.

Second, the international community is in dire need of a nation that exists solely for the benefit of cats, to protect them from the vagaries of human nature.

Third, people everywhere are crying out for an imagined Community of Cute in the midst of a world gone mad.

The owner folds up his list and declares the Republic of Cat Cafe to be the greatest utopian project in the history of mankind.

'Is this a marketing stunt?' I ask. 'I mean, to create an actual nation you'd need your own territory, right?'

I'm pretty certain that the land on which this cafe stands, in the busiest part of Strathfield, is territory that Australia is unlikely to give up any time soon.

'I pay the rent,' says the man. 'Renting is basically owning.'

Although wobbly on his territorial claim, the cafe owner has thought of everything else. He's surprisingly well-prepared. He has a cartoon flag and coat of arms ready, both emblazoned with the motto 'Community of Cute'. He has boxes filled with hot-pink Cat Cafe passports and newly minted Cat Cafe coins.

The national anthem, in Japanese, is a bouncy super-cute pop song. The owner plays it on the sound system as he trots around the cafe introducing the members of cat royalty, one by one.

'Princess Mittens, Lady Mumbles, Duchess Ragamuffin ...'

Once he's done, he turns to the humans in the cafe.

'You are all citizens of the Republic of Cat Cafe,' he shouts. His shout is positively Hitlerian.

'Will we have to pay taxes?' I ask.

'We're a tax heaven.'

'How are you going to defend the Republic? Do you have an army?'

'I *am* the army,' he shouts.

He strides to the front door and locks it. He takes a large knife from the kitchen and installs himself at the cafe entrance.

'You're either with us or against us,' he shouts. 'I henceforth declare a state of martial law.'

'Can you really enforce cuteness using violence?' I ask.

I realise I'm the only citizen in the cafe asking questions. The Republic's population comprises me, in funereal black, and a bunch of other Asian girls in pretty polka-dot rompers. They're regulars and appear to be untroubled by the owner's crazed proclamations. They like the idea of hanging here for free – a newly declared perk of citizenship – so are on board with the whole project. Besides, the three hours they've already paid for, flying by at a rate of eighteen dollars an hour including complimentary drink, aren't up yet.

'From now on,' shouts the owner, 'tourists will be required to apply a week in advance for a visa to visit the Republic of Cat Cafe.' He holds up the self-inking stamp he intends to use on foreign passports. The stamp is in the shape of a cartoon cat wearing a military uniform and a handlebar moustache.

'Hang on,' I say. 'You can't secede right now. I'm meeting a friend. How's he going to get in?'

'But you've been waiting here for hours,' says the owner.

'So?'

'Sorry to break it to you. But you've been stood up.'

It only dawns on me now, after two slices of Meow Meow Mud Cake and three Longhair Lattes and a Cutiepie Cupcake and a large bowl of Napoleon Nachos, that Michael, my best friend, might not be coming.

The owner and his knife settle down on a stool by the front door. Activity in the cafe continues as normal.

This is my first time here. To get in, you have to leave your shoes at the door. It's a bright space with a skylight, and the walls are decorated with cat murals in pastel colours. Attached to the walls are baskets and play equipment for the cats. Plush cat houses and cat-sized four-poster beds lie scattered around the floor. The cafe soundtrack is a mix of bossa nova and Yo-Yo Ma, with a slow jazz cover of 'My Favorite Things' recurring every half-hour or so.

The cute Asian girls with their dainty pink feet pursue the cats around the cafe, trying to get the perfect photo.

'Lady Cookie,' they coo. 'Lady Cooo-kiiiie.'

When in need of a rest, they return to their assigned coffee tables. They sit on cushions on the floor, drinking tea, pecking at desserts, taking selfies. They snap themselves wearing cat ears and cat masks, doing peace signs. One girl takes at least a hundred photos of herself hugging her pouting face against a pillow that has been digitally printed with the face of a Siamese cat.

After exhausting their selfie options, the girls ask me to take photos of them with the cats. I oblige, keeping their faces out of frame. The results confuse them.

Having watched everyone for the past two hours, I have come to the conclusion that, secession or no secession, the cafe is a special kind of hell for cats.

It isn't that I even care about cats: I have zero interest in them. It's just that they clearly aren't having a good time.

None of the girls seem to notice that the cats keep trying to get as far away from them as possible. They've abandoned their play equipment and beds, and are waiting near the door, in the hope that they can make a dash for it. The girls creep up to the cats and squat over them, shoving their iPhones and full-frame DSLRs in their faces.

'Hey,' I tell the owner. 'You want to secede from Australia? These cats want to secede from your cafe!'

He responds by pressing a button on a remote control. An instrumental version of 'The Girl from Ipanema' starts playing.

If the Cat Cafe is hell for cats, it's some sort of suspended reality for sweet young girls. They're all so distracted by the cuteness of the cats, they don't even realise that they – like everyone else ever born – are slowly dying.

This is how they are passing their allotted time, drinking tea and eating cake in a place that reeks of cat.

I sit here in the newly announced cat republic thinking about the first time I met Michael.

I was at university, in the first lecture of a unit called World Politics.

The lecturer was introducing us to neorealism, a theory of international relations first expounded by a man called Kenneth Waltz. The lecturer had a sonorous voice and a Scottish accent. I was entranced.

'In this course you'll be learning about several theories of international relations,' the lecturer had said. 'But the most seductive one by far is Waltzian neorealism. Why? Because of its stunning parsimony. What do I mean by parsimony? I mean that this theory is a veritable striptease. Right before your eyes, it strips the complexity of international politics down to one determining factor: the anarchic international system.'

He paused for effect. 'And what do I mean by the anarchic international system?' He paced two steps to the right, then two to the left. 'Imagine, if you will, the Hobbesian "state of nature". The great man, Thomas Hobbes, argued that before the modern nation-state came into being, there was a state of nature where all men were at war with each other. Why was this the case? Because no man had security. There was no higher coercive authority like the state to which a man could agree to give up his freedom in return for security.

'Similarly, in the international system, there is no powerful world government – merely anarchy. So states find themselves in a situation just like that of Hobbes's poor, insecure men. Without security, and with the threat of war ever present, states must reject cooperation and only help themselves. In order to survive in this realm of violence, states must compete against each other, pursuing their own interests.

'The best way to think about this is to imagine that nation-states are like billiard balls bumping around against each other within an anarchic realm, where it's every state for itself.'

As he spoke, I began to feel an incredible elation. Every cell in my body vibrated. My mind cleared. It left my body and rose above the heads of the students in the lecture theatre. I saw suddenly that if I could deduce the elegant, parsimonious theory of every aspect of life – not just of the international system – I could solve the hitherto unsolvable world.

A phone rang somewhere near the front of the lecture theatre, jolting me out of my reverie. We looked around for the culprit.

'Whoopsy daisies, it's mine,' said the lecturer. He picked up a banana yellow mobile phone and walked out.

No one knew what to do. I introduced myself to the student next to me. His name was Michael.

The lecturer returned.

'That was the Prime Minister,' he said. 'I'm babysitting his Persian cat while he's in Sweden. I hate cats. This particular cat is called Tickles. The Prime Minister wanted to inform me that Tickles has a discerning palate. Tickles eats just one flavour in the Kitty Supreme Deluxe Premium range. You will all be pleased to know that the favoured flavour is Lobster Mornay.'

I sat next to Michael for the rest of the semester.

Michael was extremely good-looking. He had the aura and academic transcript of a person who was going places. He was perfect. The only problem was that Michael was perfect in the eyes of many, and divided his attention accordingly.

Now, ten years after university, Michael works for the United Nations in New York. The woman he's marrying, from Brussels, is an intern there.

He flew back to Sydney for his engagement party last year, which was held in a restaurant overlooking the harbour.

They had neglected to put me on the guest list at the door. Embarrassed, his aunt wrote my name at the bottom of the list and added a neat tick next to it.

I was slotted in at a table of couples from the United Nations who had flown in from all over the world – handsome people who spoke in flawless sentences and drank

Moët like water. They talked about the bureaucratic politics of their agencies, and compared notes on their experiences in Tegucigalpa and Monrovia and Vientiane. They complained about how difficult it was, practically and emotionally, to have to travel for work two hundred days out of every year.

Unable to contribute to the discussion, I memorised the menu.

Later, I sidled into a conversation Michael was having at another table. He looked at me with mild surprise, as if he had not really expected me to turn up to the party. He asked what I was up to these days.

I told him I had a casual job doing mail-outs for my local council.

'Do you supervise a team of some sort?'

'No,' I said. 'I fold brochures and put them in envelopes.'

'Oh,' he said, eyes wandering.

'They're making me redundant, though. They've invented a robot that can do it all instead.'

His fiancée glided over and introduced herself.

'I went to uni with this guy!' I told her. 'Remember the time Lippman answered that call about the Prime Minister's cat?'

'We took one undergraduate class together in first year,' Michael explained.

'You should absolutely come and visit us in New York,' she said. 'We have a spare room in our apartment. You are *always* welcome. We *love* visitors. If you like cats, you can meet our two gorgeous Abyssinians. Michael and I text each other snaps of them doing the most adorable things.'

'You'll have to excuse us for a minute,' Michael said, guiding her away, two fingers on the small of her back.

Michael is back in Sydney visiting family.

We were meant to meet at 10 a.m.

It's past lunchtime.

The owner of the cafe sits at the door, with a kitchen knife in one hand and now a fire extinguisher in the other, jibing me about being stood up.

'Maybe he was in an accident,' I say.

'Face it,' he says. 'He forgot you.'

One of the girls says I should check Facebook to see when he was last active.

He liked a link posted four minutes ago by UNDF.

An idiot I found on a dating website once said to me, 'You and I, we're creating memories. Creating memories is crucial to maintaining strong relationships. We have to tend to this love like topiary.'

He wasn't a gardener.

We'd be on a roller-coaster at Luna Park, or lying on a picnic blanket staring at clouds, and he'd turn to me and say, 'What a memory!' Then he'd point at his temple and say, 'I'm filing it away up here.'

He talked incessantly about marriage and making babies.

'Everyone needs a support team,' he'd say. 'That's why people have families. They are literally creating their own teams. You and I, we're in the same league. Don't you want to be on my team? Don't you want to be a team player?'

Time passes quickly in the cat cafe.

I fall into a stupor I can't seem to escape.

In my stupor, I'm back in that lecture theatre in first year, at the very second the lecturer answers that call about the Prime Minister's cat. The lecture comes to an end. While Michael and the other students pack their bags and go forth into the world, I am the only one who remains behind, wondering why anyone would want to keep living in a world that is ultimately anarchical, and trying to reconcile the chaos of the international realm with that of a highly intelligent man agreeing to babysit a spoilt cat.

How did this factor into the parsimonious theory of life?

My stupor goes on for a day, then two days, then a week, then a month.

One morning I cast it aside to discover that the owner, scared of losing a citizen, has been pouring a liquidised mix of carrot cake and potato salad down my throat to keep my body working.

'It was the most nutrient-rich food available in the Republic,' he says when I wake. 'Feeding you was like fattening up a foie gras duck.'

Fresh from my stupor, I discover that the owner's secession movement has begun to depart dramatically from its original intent.

Realising that his micronation lacks natural resources, the owner has resorted to tourism as a main source of national income. He has started operating a backpackers' hostel upstairs, complete with a pool table and a karaoke machine.

The first backpackers to arrive present their passports and dump their backpacks at the door of the Republic.

'Phwoar,' the men say, ogling the girls in the cafe as much as the cats. They did not expect to encounter such cute young things here.

Tourism in the Republic soon ramps up. The girls, enjoying the attention but wanting even more, request plastic surgery to maximise their cuteness. The owner agrees to pay a surgeon to visit the Republic. The surgeon helps the girls grow cat ears and cat tails, so that they can out-cute their feline friends.

'I don't understand,' I say to them. 'What is happening?'

'Analysis is paralysis,' the girls reply as they climb off the operating tables. 'Go with the flow.'

Surgery over, they strut the floor of the Republic swishing their new tails. They curl up in the laps of the backpackers. They brush the backpackers' cheeks with their cat whiskers.

Increasing numbers of men flood in. In addition to the backpackers, a large cohort of awkward, pallid men arrive, travelling the world for some exotic loving. They have heard about the strange 'sexy-cuteness' of the citizens of the Republic, and have come to see what all the fuss is about.

The men get drunk on a mix of vodka and Red Bull, which the owner has recently added to the beverage list. Panting, they chase the cat girls around the cafe.

The place becomes a destination not just for tourism but also for sex tourism – an arena of titillation, with per-hour pricing for petting in the rooms upstairs.

The owner continues to sit at the front door, encouraging

the girls now and then with two thumbs up. He busies himself with stamping his military cat on anything and everything, and delighting in the mounting piles of cash from visitors passing in and out of the cat nation.

Now that the girls are far cuter than the cats, they realise that the cats have become redundant. The cats are using up precious food and space. The cats aren't earning their keep.

The girls divide the cats into two groups. They skin the first group and wear the fur around their necks. The second group is taxidermied for the planned Museum of the Republic of Cat Cafe, which is to feature an exhibit charting the physical evolution of the Republic's citizenry.

The remaining flesh is cooked on a portable spit and served to guests with a side of nachos.

The girls take the names of the cats. I am forced to start calling fully-grown humans Duchess Ragamuffin and Lady Mumbles.

After the last of the cats has been consumed, the Duchess points at me and then at a broom in the corner of the cafe. 'If you're too good for sex,' she says, 'you can clean.'

She tells me to start in the middle of the cafe and extend outwards in a widening spiral.

I shrug and get the broom. I guess I have nothing else to do.

'Walking meditation will be good for your troubled mental state,' says Lady Mumbles, 'as well as for the general upkeep of the Republic.'

As I sweep, I try to work out the parsimonious theory of the Cat Cafe. It's a real mess.

A month of waiting turns into a year.

The owner takes to standing outside the entrance of the cafe on a milk crate to drum up even more business.

Two policemen show up. Someone has alerted them to a man with wild eyes loitering in front of a cafe asking passers-by to apply for visas to his imaginary nation, and threatening them with a fire extinguisher when they refuse.

'What do you think you're doing?' one of the policemen asks the owner. He points to the cafe. 'Is this your establishment?'

The owner asks to see their passports. He won't talk to them unless he sees a valid visa.

'Be serious,' says one of the officers. 'You could be in a lot of trouble here, mate.'

'What?' says the owner. 'Are you going to invade my Community of Cute?'

He picks up the fire extinguisher and holds it above his head with both hands. He charges at the policemen, declaring war on Australia.

'Never seen a Chinese terrorist before,' says one, dodging him.

We watch from the cafe as the policemen subdue the owner and take him away.

For the first time ever, I am alone with the stupid cat girls. I put down my broom and sit quietly with them on the floor of the cafe, staring at all the dead cats. The girls look stunned, as if only just realising we've all been held hostage for a year.

I suggest that it's time for us to abandon this place. That this could be our chance to leave behind the failures of the Republic and to resume our previous lives.

'But we have nowhere to go,' say the cat girls. 'Haven't you noticed no one's come looking for us, wondering where we've been?'

'I've got nowhere to go either,' I say. 'At least you have each other, in your own murderous bubble of cuteness.'

They purr and lick my hand.

I tell them that I am lonely. I tell them this is probably because I still don't understand the parsimonious theory of friendship.

'Think bigger, my friend,' says an unfamiliar voice. The voice belongs to a taxidermied tabby sitting in one of the baskets nailed to the wall. 'First you have to understand the parsimonious theory of your life. That theory is simple. You want everyone else to be perfect. But take a look at yourself. You're a nutcase who turns up to lectures and parties without being invited. Accept that you yourself are completely stuffed, and you won't feel so alone. Obviously, you're shit at friendships. But you could be good at the opposite of friendship. After all, your key personal strength is going places where you aren't welcome. Embrace anarchy. Move into bigger territories. Annex some shit. There are two kinds of people in this world – power-makers and power-takers. Which kind are you?'

The tabby is making a lot of sense. I jump to my feet.

'Where are you going?' ask the cat girls.

'I'm seceding from the Republic. I'm starting a micro-nation called the Republic of the Parsimonious Theory of

Cat Cafe. I'm the new President.'

I point at the taxidermied tabby. 'Your new name is Kenneth Waltz. You're coming with me.'

'Fine,' she says.

I tuck her under one arm. 'Let's play pool.'

The cat girls secede with us.

Upstairs, the backpackers, fresh from afternoon naps, breathe down our necks, their fingers reaching out to stroke.

Princess Mittens produces the kitchen knife. She slaughters them all.

One falls lifeless across the pool table, spurting blood, sinking the eight ball.

The cat girls hiss. They pull the body off the table.

I wipe the blood from the eight ball and reposition it.

I execute the break shot and watch where the balls roll.

Inquiry Regarding the Recent
Goings-On in the Woods

Introduction

We had a number of requests from the public to review the recent goings-on in the woods. These requests voiced the grievances of members of the local village – grievances we take extremely seriously.

Concerns

Many villagers did not appreciate the way the woods made them feel.

I hear a pounding at night, wrote one villager, *like someone is galloping through the undergrowth. But when I look, I can't see anyone.*

Every time I go in there, wrote another, *it sounds like I'm being stalked by a serial killer.*

Fairies, wrote yet another. *That incessant tinkling gives me the shits.*

This collective concern about the woods was not unfounded. Our investigations suggested, however, that the classes of suspects identified in the letters were not the sources of the auditory disruptions. Instead, we discovered that the forest was harbouring an exiled Russian orchestra, which had made a pastime of accompanying visitors through the woods.

Background

Older folk in the village were not surprised.

'The conductor was the start of the troubles,' said an old woman with a beard. 'He arrived in the village with just a stick. Not even a suitcase! Kept waving his arms round like a lunatic. One day, he went into the woods. We didn't see him again. Probably pointing that bloody stick at the woodpeckers.'

'Sounds like he's gathered up forces,' said an old man behind her, his arms folded over vast, flat breasts. They nodded in unison.

'I should warn you now.' The old woman shook her finger at the Review Committee. 'You must never look into the eyes of a musician.'

'Or what?' asked one of the Committee members, a nervous young man.

But the woman had already shuffled off into the background and we all scribbled on our notepads that the young man's question had been lost to the wind.

Definition

We resolved that the public was not obliged to tolerate the guerilla orchestra. Our reasoning was as follows:

1. By definition, the woods were a collection of trees.
2. The official function of a collection of trees was neither:
   a. the confusion of local citizens; nor
   b. the withdrawal of 'musicians' from the productive economy.

Offensive Strategies

(A)

At first, we tried to smoke the Russians out. We waited from daybreak until the moon was up but no one emerged. By midnight, all that was emanating from the woods was bawdy laughter and dirty jazz.

Intelligence later came through that members of the orchestra, particularly the woodwind players, were mighty fond of smoking.

On hearing this, the President of the Committee punched a tree.

He had always been an overly dramatic man. Decades ago, his presidential office was conferred on him as punishment for attempting to run down his wife's lover with a tractor. This attempt had been unsuccessful because the top speed of the tractor could not match the top speed of its prospective victim. The magistrate had been so appalled by the man's lack of foresight on this point that he condemned him to a lifetime of reviewing on request the wayward actions of fellow villagers.

But we digress. This time, we note, the President's run-in with the tree was somewhat warranted. He had also just been informed that his daughter had eloped from the family home. A fresh trail of cigarette butts led from the President's doorstep to the forest entrance.

(B)

By sunrise, a dare had materialised around the edges of the woods in the form of a perfect white chalk circle.

The musicians were taunting us.

They knew that wherever there was a line we would want to cross it.

(C)

'Cover!' screamed the President.

We dove behind trees and cowered there until it became clear that the orchestra was merely feigning a battle scene. Drums raged, violins were on the attack and cymbals hung about like snipers. All we had walked into was a harmless musical ambush.

We were being mocked by a guerilla orchestra and we didn't like it one bit.

The musicians changed tack with a Gilbert and Sullivan retrospective. Some of our men, who had joined the Committee to meet other men, couldn't help themselves. Suddenly they were Modern Major-Generals, pinafored sailors and petite Japanese maids. The noise from their dancing and singing impeded our advance, so the decision was made to sedate them. We left them strewn all over the forest, creating the impression that we had assassinated the cast of a musical mashup.

'Success is within reach,' declared the President at sunset, despite all evidence to the contrary. But he was struck immediately by an incredible yawn. The rest of us fell about yawning sympathetically and were all soon in a pile, fast asleep, in the midst of a lullaby.

(D)

Dawn lit up the thousands of gramophones we had placed at regular intervals around the chalk circle.

We had mustered the village's entire supply of music-playing devices.

This was possible due to the villagers' complete support of our new strategy. To them, the sound of a French horn was a threat. They liked only the sounds with which they were familiar. The village butcher was in charge of maintaining a centralised list of favoured sounds, which he kept for public viewing in a small ledger in the community hall.

Among the sounds with solid followings in the village were those of:
- forms of transport, such as tractors; and
- beer gushing from the tap in the local pub.

We began the siege at seven o'clock in the morning, confident that the gramophones would deafen our opponents and render them unable to prepare new accompaniments for combat. The din was almost unbearable but we persisted. After all, we were striking at the heart of the orchestra's tactics.

By lunchtime, however, the villagers were cursing the

very invention of the gramophone. They filed an official request that we rid them forever of their musical devices.

Once our gramophonic inferno had subsided to a slow burn, the orchestra returned fire with a rendition of Beethoven's ninth symphony.

(E)

Equipment dwindling, we started to create more effective ammunition. Our key strategy was to compose scathing reviews of the orchestra and nail them to the trees at the outskirts of the woods. The reviews contained remarks such as:

These people are testament to the fact that just because you can count to twelve doesn't mean you should play an instrument.

And:

Attending a performance by this lot is worse than listening to a site of builders drilling and farting.

Then the President of the Committee picked up a loud-speaker and repeated for an entire day and night the bullet points set out on a piece of paper he had prepared earlier. The document contained the following assertions:

- *Musicians are failed professionals.*
- *A real musician never hides behind an orchestra.*
- *We are concerned that some of you are experiencing depressive tendencies because your lives are useless.*
- *We note that today is Are You Coping Day and we are wondering if You Are Coping. You may wish to avail yourself of a number of brochures on mental health that are currently in our possession.*

A bassoonist, long plagued with guilt about his membership of the group, gave himself up. The second he crossed the chalk line we swaddled him in blankets and took him to the nearest accounting firm, where he was put in a sharp suit and tie and placed in the next Excellerate intake.

(F)

For immunity and a favourable salary package, the bassoonist had marked on our map the locations of the pits where the rest of the orchestra was hiding.

We donned noise-cancelling earmuffs and fanned out. Our priority was to pick off the double bass players: even with their instruments strapped to their backs, they moved slower than the rest.

We sawed our trophy instruments into pieces and added them to the gramophones, listening to their dying melodic crackle as we warmed our hands against the fire.

(G)

Gradually, we hunted the orchestra down to a chamber orchestra. Then a quintet. A quartet. A trio, then a duo.

In the end, just one musician was left. A member of the second violins.

We circled him in a clearing. There was now a chalk circle surrounding the woods and a concentric human circle at its heart.

The violinist wore an open shirt and a gold medallion that nestled on his white chest hair. We disliked his flamboyant dress sense and his insufferable attitude.

'So what?' he said. 'I will be a great soloist.'

We broke his violin against a tree.

'So I will sing,' he said.

We cut off his ears.

'So I have perfect pitch.'

We took out his voice box.

He started to conduct in 3/4 time.

We severed his arms.

He tried to dance a jig.

We crushed his legs and strung him up by the neck with his violin strings.

Results

Recalling the old woman's warning, the President of the Committee ordered us to turn away from the scene after our work was done. But the nervous young Committee member, whose question had been lost to the wind, climbed a ladder so he could look into the violinist's eyes.

We heard the young man begin to cry.

Then we heard a shot.

He had put the barrel of his gun into his own mouth.

I retreated from the woods wearing my earmuffs.

I could not listen to the silence.

Conclusion

A week later, we cut down the corpse of the violinist and gave it a funeral, which we had decided was the right thing to do in so tragic a situation as this. We even imported the sister from a neighbouring village for the occasion.

Upon our strong suggestion, the woman lamented to the congregation the day her brother had first picked up the violin, as the instrument had been the direct cause of his death.

Prior to the burial, we were inundated with letters from members of the public requesting a funeral march, which they thought appropriate to commemorate their grief upon the unfortunate death of the violinist. We were unable to meet these requests as we had exhausted the village's supply of gramophones and instrumentalists. We planned to substitute the funeral march with a choral work but realised during the procession that none of the Review Committee members knew how to sing.

The debacle drew the infinite anger of the public. In response to our disrespectful conduct, every one of their initial requests for a review of the woods was withdrawn and alternative requests issued.

We question the necessity of the most recent goings-on in the woods, said one letter, *in light of the almost total massacre last year of a troupe of ink and wash artists in exile from China, who were, in fact, those responsible for painting the woods into existence with the intention of providing the villagers with a space for spiritual escape.*

The alternative requests demanded to know how the eradication of the Russian orchestra had occurred, which is the subject of the present inquiry.

Recommendation

We are at pains to emphasise that the key figures responsible for the recent goings-on in the woods must be brought to justice.

Our suspicions as to their continued existence are based on investigations into a further request from a villager still uncomfortable with the way the woods have been making him feel.

I hear a pounding at night, he complains, *like someone is galloping through the undergrowth. But when I look, I can't see anyone.*

Testimonials have confirmed sightings of a black ink horse moving in sync with a galloping bass drum, under the combined spell of a master brush and a master baton.

The Procession

The three-year-old is sucking on a lollipop.

He's the size of a fully-grown man. His hair is shaved up the sides, culminating in a topknot tied with a big red bow. He's dressed in his best yellow silk robes, which have been embroidered with elaborate green dragons and red tractors.

The three-year-old wants to be at the head of the birthday procession. The other gods aren't so sure. After all, it isn't his birthday, it's someone else's. The gods mutter among themselves in their strange, high-pitched language.

Finally, they give in.

The drumming starts. Gongs sound. Cymbals clash. Whistles thrill the air.

The three-year-old cracks his whip and takes the lead. He skips forth, arms pumping, leading the parade of birthday floats with their blinking lights down the dark, muggy streets of Klang.

Fat gods and thin gods, tall gods and short. Each walks behind a neon float, followed by an entourage.

Along comes the God of Lost Things. His float is a ute piled high with bric-a-brac. Abandoned children sit among the junk, smiling and clapping, their feet hanging off the back of the vehicle. They laugh and point at the Goddess of Old Maids, who charges ahead in a white veil and dress, looking as if she has come straight from the altar.

Wandering after her is the Immortal Priestess of Mild, Moderate and Gross Injustices. She seems lost, wearing a blindfold and carrying a set of digital scales she can't read.

The monkey god flips forward and back, light as air.

The tiger god lopes along, growling. Now and then he claws at the scratching post installed at the back of his float.

'There,' says Ben. He points to a float at the rear of the procession. 'That's the one I'm here to see. They call him the Economist.'

The Economist is a serious-looking guy with a boring haircut. Like Ben, he's wearing a suit.

'He seems ordinary,' I say.

Ben shakes his head. 'You're pretty but so naïve. If the most powerful god in the world knocked on your door and sat down at your kitchen table, you wouldn't even realise.'

I fold my arms and stare at my bare feet. Ben never lets me into this car unless I take off my sandals. This car is his beloved. It's a souped-up white BMW with black rims and doors that open vertically.

We're parked on the side of the street, watching the parade. Ben has driven us here straight after work, rap songs about bitches and hoes blaring from the car's audio system. He's adjusted the bass so it's as loud as possible – it thumps right through the chest.

The whole way over here, Ben kept boasting about the latest multi-million-dollar deal he's closed at the bank, and how, going forward, he's going to upgrade to a new matt-black BMW. He'll upgrade once he marries me, he decides out loud.

He says he deserves it.

I curl up against the car window and watch the parade more closely. I want to find something that can distract me from Ben's voice, which is now lecturing me about the fact that marriage is a beautiful invention, created so that a man and a woman can pool financial resources and buy property together.

A small dog, white with light brown patches, darts through the crowd. Captivated, I watch its tiny zigzag until it disappears from view.

The Economist's entourage is much longer than all the other entourages put together. It goes on for blocks. His float is a stretch limousine with a screen mounted on top, displaying a slideshow populated with ever-shifting graphs that track share prices and interest rates rising and falling in real time.

An old man is at the front of the entourage begging the Economist for a forecast.

'He's a finance minister,' Ben explains.

The Economist walks along with his eyes rolled into the back of his head. An assistant hurries after him with a parasol, as if shielding the Economist from some unknown danger.

Through a megaphone, the Economist speaks of the endless good works of the Invisible Hand, the all-knowing power of the Market.

He takes a sword from another assistant and draws the blade across his tongue. He lets the blood drip onto the tip of a paintbrush, then uses it to write a forecast for the minister on yellow paper.

Once it's done, he turns to his entourage. He sticks out his tongue.

The cut has healed. Everyone gasps.

At the very end of the procession is a sweaty, potbellied man in a brown patchwork coat. The coat hangs loose at the neckline, leaving one nipple exposed. The man clutches a fan in one hand and a gourd-shaped bottle in the other. He stumbles along, barefoot and giggling, his eyes half-closed.

'Look at that drunk shit,' says Ben. 'Probably homeless.'

The drunk turns to look at us, as if he has heard. He cocks his head and smiles. Pendulums of saliva stretch from his mouth. Swaying, he takes a red carnation from inside his coat and beckons us with it.

Ben sniggers. 'Be still my beating heart.'

I look at Ben, then at the drunk.

I unlock the car door.

'What are you doing?' says Ben.

The heat of the night envelops me. My feet swing out and touch the bitumen.

'Are you nuts? What about your shoes?'

I hurry over to the drunk. He takes a swig from his gourd then sprays the mouthful of liquid into the air. A fine mist descends.

He proffers the gourd to me. I decline, smiling.

I fall into line behind him. He walks with his feet turned

out, taking steps in complicated patterns as if following the rules of some private dance.

Ben starts the car and begins to trail us, bringing up the rear of the procession.

The Economist continues to preach through the megaphone. To demonstrate a point, he calls the three-year-old over and snatches the lollipop from the child's mouth.

He snaps his fingers. The lollipop shoots into the air and multiplies. Thousands of lollipops rain down over the crowd. People crawl over each other to get at the sweets. They scratch and slap. They tear out each other's hair.

In the stampede, a woman screams.

'Oh! The dog! The poor little dog!'

The back of the procession halts.

The drunk pushes through the crowd and stumbles in the direction of the woman's voice. I follow.

Arriving at the spot, we discover the little brown and white dog lying sprawled on the ground. There isn't any blood but its body has been completely crushed, trampled by the crowd.

'Who owns this animal?' asks the Economist of the crowd. He points at the limp, broken body.

The dog looks up at me, its eyes full of shock.

The drunk crouches over the dog and wipes its tears away. He strokes its matted hair. He comforts it with gentle, unintelligible words. He plants a kiss on its head, picks it up, tucks it under one arm, and proceeds past the Economist's float.

The brawl resumes.

Having returned to the head of the procession, the three-year-old takes a sudden turn into a wire-fenced parking lot.

Although he has lost his lollipop, he has somehow gained a replacement dummy.

Sucking happily on his new acquisition, he skips across the vacant lot towards the back fence, accelerating.

As he nears the fence, he steps up into the air.

The procession follows, moving along an invisible plane that extends over the fence and above the palm trees.

The drunk does the same.

I hesitate.

Ben's voice calls out. It booms. He seems to have wangled a megaphone from someone in the parade.

'Lex, are you getting a lift back, or what?'

The drunk looks down at me and grins.

'Birthday,' he trills. 'Mine. Come to party?'

The dog yaps and wags its tail.

I smile.

I step forward and up.

Above the trees, I look back at the Economist's float. The driver revs the engine. The float speeds full tilt towards the fence.

It crashes through.

The crowd heaves around it, still fighting.

I spot Ben hanging out the window of his car, peering up at me. The car is stuck behind the float, unable to move – a white speck in the raging crush.

I laugh.

I'll never have to sit in that souped-up piece of junk again.

I wave to my shoes and send them a farewell kiss.
I swing my arms. The drums roll.
Stepping up above the city, we march on.

The Sister Company

Orla had been doing well in the session up until the point where the young Thai masseuse who called herself Rabbit asked her to sit up and cross her legs.

Orla did as she was told. Rabbit squatted behind her and began digging her elbow into the back of Orla's shoulder. Orla held the towel over her breasts with one hand, and bowed her head. That's when she began to cry. The tears dripped right into her lap.

Rabbit stopped. 'I make you hurt?'

'It's not you,' said Orla. 'Just another bad day.'

'I go on?' said Rabbit.

Orla wiped the tears from her eyes, nodding. She concentrated on the sound of the bamboo flute filtering through the room. Rabbit pushed her knees against Orla's back and placed her hands on either side of Orla's jaw. She stretched Orla's head up and back, making her spine arch. She finished by clapping her hands all over Orla's back.

'Done,' she said.

She slipped out and slid the door closed.

Orla felt dizzy as she got off the table. Her body smelled like massage oil and Tiger Balm. The room didn't have a mirror but Orla knew her hair was all messed up. She pulled out the elastic and tried to flatten the stray strands as best she could. She also knew there'd be an embarrassing towel imprint on her chin and cheeks but there was nothing she could do about that.

Out in the waiting room, Rabbit had made a cup of green tea for her to drink.

Underneath the cup was a business card.

'For you,' said Rabbit.

The card was thick and white, bearing capital letters embossed in blue.

THE SISTER COMPANY, it said. *THERAPY, LIFE COACHING & COMPANIONSHIP FOR THE MELANCHOLIC.*

Below the capital letters was a phone number.

★

In the days following the massage, Orla had trouble getting out of bed in the morning. It didn't help that the sky had been dark for three weeks of summer thunderstorms, with no end in sight.

She still managed to get to work on time each day. It was standing room only on the train. She swayed with the rest of the passengers, one hand gripping the nearest pole, and the other thrust into her trouser pocket, fingertips pressing against the corners of the business card that Rabbit had given her.

She wondered how she had become so lonely. Boring, bawling Orla – the one everyone left behind.

By the time Christmas Eve rolled around, Orla still hadn't called the Sister Company. During the morning commute, she slipped her hand into her pocket and noticed the corners of the card were bent and soft. She'd have to make the call soon, before the whole card disintegrated.

Work was a tiny office in a building on York Street in the CBD. The company Orla worked for shared the first floor with a small-time wills and estates law firm. It was quiet in the office when Orla arrived – all the other content writers were already hooked up at their desks, their eyes closed.

Orla hooked in to her own set of neurobuds, closed her eyes, and started working again on the simulation on her task list.

She sat there developing a new scene, visualising a naked woman having an erotic moment on a horse. She added details to the visualisation: full breasts, hardening nipples, a red heart locket around the woman's neck. She made the horse bare its teeth.

Then her focus wavered and she began thinking about buying an ice-cream on her lunch break. A soft serve cone suddenly materialised in the woman's hand. In the woman's other hand appeared a business card with blue capital letters.

Shit, thought Orla, and deleted the two details.

She rewound the draft in her mind and began working the angles. She started the visualisation again from the point of view of the woman. And then from the point of view of the horse. For every sim, there was always at least one weirdo who wrote in asking to experience the POV of the incidental fauna.

'How's the story going?' The face of Orla's boss flashed up on the interface to her right.

'All right,' said Orla.

'How many hours has it taken?'

'Twenty so far. I'm up to chapter six.'

'Well, the budget's thirty-five. So don't get bogged down. No political intrigue, please. I know how you get. We're producing erotica, not *Richard III*.'

'Sure thing.'

'The client's looking for an eighty per cent job. They're not paying for perfection. We need to send it to sound design by end of Boxing Day.'

'No worries.'

'Anyway, remember the *Rising Tide* sim you wrote the other month?'

Orla nodded but couldn't remember. Maybe it was the one about the sea monster with six penises.

'It outsold expectations by ten thousand. When you focus, Orla, you seem to have a finger on what the ladies want.'

'Oh,' said Orla. 'Great.'

It didn't feel great. Nothing felt great anymore. Orla couldn't even remember the last time she really laughed.

'We're having after-work drinks with that client, first Wednesday after New Year,' said her boss. 'A bit of a celebration. Put it in your calendar. And, you know, try and wear some make-up for it. Spruce yourself up a bit.'

'Will do.'

'Can't believe Christmas is tomorrow. The year flew by. What are you getting up to?'

'Lunch,' said Orla. 'Maybe.'

'Sorry I didn't get around to organising a Christmas party. Working mother, juggling balls, trying to have it all, et cetera.'

'Not a problem.'

Orla's boss flicked off screen.

Orla locked her workstation and left.

As she made her way to Town Hall Station, a stream of people pushed past her. They were dressed in suspenders and fedoras and fishnets and feather headpieces and long strings of pearls. They piled into white minibuses that were parked in a chain up the street, ready to be driven off to their themed Christmas party.

Orla watched them flirt and giggle. They all wished they were in the Roaring Twenties, she thought, but instead they were living lives in which their bosses dictated to them what to wear on the one day a year assigned for workplace shenanigans.

Orla pulled the business card out of her pocket. She called the number.

'Can I have your earliest available appointment?'

★

The closest branch of the Sister Company was in a narrow building on George Street, next to Wynyard Station. According to the building directory, it was the only office on the second floor. Orla shook the rain off her umbrella and took the lift.

The office was small, with bright red furniture and grey carpet. A small peace lily in a white ceramic pot sat on one side of the reception desk.

A middle-aged woman behind the desk looked up from some filing.

'I'm here for a twelve o'clock appointment?' said Orla.

The receptionist blinked. She ran one red nail over the pencilled entries in a one-day-to-a-page diary. There was something slightly mechanical about the way she moved, a waxy shine to her face.

'Orla?'

'That's me.'

'I'm Rhonda. Merry Christmas.'

'I was surprised you're open on Christmas Day.'

'The wellbeing of our clients is more important to us than public holidays. So, it seems you're here to do a pre-session with us.'

'Uh huh.'

'Please,' said Rhonda. 'Come this way.'

Orla followed the receptionist down a corridor. The office extended further back than she thought it would. She looked at the back of Rhonda's wig-like hair, watched the stiff swing of her arm, and noticed the little lag in her feet as she walked. It finally dawned on her.

'Sorry, Rhonda?'

'Yes?' Rhonda turned.

'This is the first time I've met an android in real life.'

'Not as scary as you thought, right?'

'It's kind of cool.'

Rhonda smiled. There was lipstick on her teeth but Orla decided not to mention it. Orla thought Rhonda's smile looked fake. Maybe that was just an unavoidable consequence of having a fake mouth.

'As the controlling company of your employer,' said Rhonda, 'the Parent Company has a mental health scheme in place by which it will fully subsidise you for six initial sessions with the Sister Company.'

'Wow. That really helps.'

'I don't know why your boss didn't put you on the scheme directly.'

'I don't talk about my private life at work.'

'I see,' said Rhonda. 'And we're here.'

She opened a door and ushered Orla into a dark room. In the room stood a tall black box.

'I know.' Rhonda rolled her eyes. 'It looks like a coffin. We have cutting-edge tech but idiot designers. You don't have claustrophobia, do you?'

'I don't think so.'

'When I close this door, you'll find yourself in complete darkness. Don't be alarmed. It's meant to be like that.'

Sure enough, when Orla stepped in and the door closed behind her, she couldn't see a thing. Whether her eyes were open or shut, all there was in front of her was pitch black.

Rhonda's voice echoed around her ears.

'Now, what we're going to do is a top-down body and brain scan. I'd like you to speak about what's been bothering you that has led you to seek therapy. The booth will be monitoring your brain activity as you speak. Start when you want to start. End when you want to end. You have all day, if you like. The more detail you can put in, the more it will assist us to tailor our therapy to your needs. When you're ready to leave the booth, just push the door open and walk back up the corridor. I'll be waiting for you at reception. Are you ready?'

'Yes,' said Orla.

'Great. Keep your eyes closed throughout the process and I'll see you on the other side.'

A low buzz replaced Rhonda's voice. Orla closed her eyes. Through her eyelids she could see a beam of light slowly moving down past her face.

She started where she wanted to start, and ended where she wanted to end. She didn't know how long she was in there but it felt like an hour, maybe two. The light seemed to move in a cycle, passing her eyelids over and over again.

When she was done, Orla fumbled in the dark for a tissue and wiped her eyes. She sat quietly for a moment before feeling for the door.

Back in reception, Rhonda smiled at her.

'How was it?'

'All right. A bit emotional.'

Orla noticed Rhonda's nostrils flare. She was yawning through her nose, as if Orla wouldn't be able to tell.

'It can be difficult,' said Rhonda, 'but it's a very brave first step to take.'

'Thanks.'

'Well, then, what we're going to do now is collate the results of your scan and I'll see you at the same time next week.'

'Oh! That's New Year's Day.'

'Are you busy?'

'No.'

'Good. It'll be a two-hour introductory session with

your therapy companion. All sessions thereafter will be one hour each.'

'Do I need to sign anything?'

'It's all taken care of.'

Orla went out into the street. She didn't feel like going back to her flat, with its one tiny room and grimy windows and cockroaches that came crawling out of nowhere.

She walked down to York Street and caught the lift up to her office.

She settled into her chair and hooked herself up. She visualised the rest of the *Equine Equinox* sim and went through to check that she'd more or less stuck to the assigned plotline. Then she printed out the list of required product placements and went through the draft again, adding an Hermès bag here, a Jeep there.

Orla was sick of it all by the time she got to the Lacoste shoes. There were still about thirty placements to go.

She unhooked herself from the desk and walked across to Town Hall. She decided to pass the rest of the day riding the train around Sydney.

The train spoke to Orla and everyone else in the carriage.

'Merry Christmas and thank you, customers, for choosing to ride with ParentRail.'

The message annoyed Orla, as it always did. She'd had no other choice.

Orla tried not to look at the ads flashing all over the floors, walls and ceilings of the carriage. It was difficult. Her eyes settled on a live-action ad showing a bunch of women with taut bodies dancing around in multicoloured underwear.

As the train passed Macdonaldtown, the carriage lights dimmed, the windows transitioned to grey, and an American celebrity hologram began moving through the carriage. The holograd started talking to the grey-haired woman next to Orla about a new cola. The holograd shimmered and held a holocan out to the woman.

'If it has zero calories, does it really exist?' asked the woman.

'Yes, indeed,' said the holograd.

'What's it like dating Judd W?'

'A gentlewoman doesn't kiss and tell,' winked the holograd. 'But what I will say is that this cola tastes like freedom.'

The woman ordered two cases on the spot to be delivered to her doorstep. The holograd scanned her wrist, confirmed the transaction and continued its virtual sashay through the carriage.

★

On New Year's Eve, Orla didn't even leave the flat. She got into her pyjamas, baked a batch of frozen chips, and turned on the NYE coverage.

Orla didn't feel like hooking in to the sim version. Having it play out in her own mind would be too much, so she watched the coverage on her old vision. She watched two blond hosts compliment each other on their tasteless fluoro dresses, dropping the names of their designers. Somehow, the women looked younger than they were last year.

'After a year of highs and lows, gains and losses,' said one, 'you deserve these fireworks, beautiful Sydney.'

'There's certainly no greater place in the world to live,' said the other.

Orla flicked through the other channels – ParentGlow, ParentTen, ParentHood. The same program was being broadcast on all of them.

Next up was a montage of hurricanes and tsunamis and scandals and elections and parades from the year that was, a few clips of 2030's hottest hits, and then the nine o'clock family fireworks, accompanied by a medley of Wagner and uberpop.

As they had been for a number of years, the fireworks were pre-programmed graphics superimposed on micro-drone footage of Sydney's landmarks. According to the government, these were cheaper and safer than actual fireworks, and kept citizens from milling around in dangerously large groups at vantage points across the city's foreshore.

The musical accompaniment and fireworks combinations varied each year, to keep the mix fresh. This time, the display opened with millions of shimmering rainbow pinwheels and dancing monkeys. Eleven cricketers in green and gold walked across the sky. A fleet of eleven silver ships sailed in the opposite direction. The smell of gunpowder wafted through the vision's olfactor.

When the last of the virtual nine o'clock fireworks had spun out over Sydney Harbour and poured golden from the Harbour Bridge, Orla turned off the vision, twisted earplugs into her ears, and went to sleep.

★

It was quiet in the CBD the morning after, as Orla made her way to her next session with the Sister Company.

Just like the week before, she took the lift.

The doors opened onto the second floor. A gangly blond woman in a sky blue dress rushed in, bumping into her.

'Fuck, sorry,' she said.

'No worries,' said Orla, stepping out.

The woman's eyes were red and puffy. She held a tissue to her nose, sniffling.

'You know how it is,' she said as the doors closed. 'Therapy dredges up the worst. But they say I'll be functional again soon.'

Orla sat in the waiting room. For a while, she watched Rhonda pottering around – refilling the business card holder, adjusting the height of her swivel chair, flicking through documents and licking her index finger now and then. Orla bowed her head and stared into her lap.

'Orla?' a woman said, in a voice that sounded precisely like her own.

'Yes?'

Orla looked up. The first thing she noticed was her therapist's black flats. They were identical to Orla's, with little shiny bows at the top. Then Orla saw the black trousers and polka-dot shirt. The therapist was wearing the exact same outfit that Orla had worn to the pre-session.

'Hola, Orla,' said the therapist. 'Happy New Year.'

The other strange thing was that the woman's face looked exactly like Orla's, minus the chubbiness. Overall, the woman was slimmer than Orla, with clearer skin. Her hair was also ash brown but without the black roots. In fact, everything that Orla hated about her own body – the fat in weird places, the heavy arms, the forearm freckles – was gone.

'How did ...' Orla took a moment to think. 'You're an android.'

'I am. My name's Kabuki.'

'As in kabuki theatre?'

'I'm Japanese tech, Australianised. The Sydney development team thought it'd be cute to name me after words they pulled out of a Tokyo guidebook. Initially I saw your name and thought you were going to be Irish.'

'I'm Chinese, Australianised. My parents named me after a brand of kitchen sponge.'

Kabuki smiled, nodding.

They shook hands. Kabuki's was surprisingly warm. It felt like real flesh and blood.

Kabuki ushered her down the corridor and into a consultation room. A bookshelf lined one wall. The shelves were mostly empty, except for three antique paperbacks, stress balls in assorted shapes and colours, a series of frosted blue vases, and a cactus in a terracotta pot.

'Don't be too overwhelmed by how realistic I appear,' said Kabuki. 'Our receptionist, Rhonda, is an earlier model. Artificially intelligent but nothing more.'

'I didn't know technology was so far along,' said Orla. 'They still can't even get the train timetable right.'

They sat down opposite each other.

'The public isn't always aware of the latest technological advancements,' Kabuki said. 'It's a matter of priorities. With money and commitment, you can make anything happen.'

She crossed her legs and clasped her hands, resting them on one knee.

'So what we're beginning today is a program of individualised therapy, which we call Integrational Realignment – a sort of early intervention with a personal touch.

'The edge I have over regular and holotherapy is that I can completely identify with your particular situation. As you recall, in the pre-session we monitored your brain activity as you recounted emotions you felt during past trauma.'

Kabuki reached behind her left ear and pulled out a microchip the size of a pea.

'The program in this chip replicates that unique mix of emotion and experience. It functions as an overlay for my essential system. It's like having a brain that can run on two tracks simultaneously. On one layer I have your lived experience, which provides me with the ability to feel exactly as you have felt. Underlying that layer is in-depth therapeutic knowhow, which I'll use to help you nurture your positive thinking. In short, what I can offer you is exceptionally tailored coaching and companionship that will help you become functional again.'

'So you understand why I made the appointment,' said Orla.

Kabuki reinserted the chip, nodding.

Orla was relieved. If Kabuki really did have full emotional capabilities, then she knew how it all felt. The weekends of interminable crying, the inordinate weight gain, the sheen disappearing from every new acquaintance and wedding and party and barbecue. She knew about Orla having no family left. About all the good friends who'd upped and moved away without bothering to leave forwarding addresses. About the guys Orla had dated who'd dropped off the radar and never called again. She literally felt how Orla felt, watching everyone around her just following the crowd, procreating, and marking time with gins on Friday nights and lattes at weekend brunches.

Kabuki smiled. 'You've lived in Sydney your whole life but you don't have much to show for it. You wonder if this is all an illusion, a nightmare. You wonder if this is a holding city, where you're just waiting to die. You're slowing down but the days are speeding up and blending into each other.'

'Shouldn't you have worse existential anxieties than I do?' asked Orla.

'I'm the therapist here,' Kabuki laughed. 'So out of the two of us I'm clearly dealing all right.'

'How do you think I should fix it?'

'You already know how,' said Kabuki. 'There's no new path to happiness. It's a choice.'

'Well, I know what people say will fix it. But I don't think it will work.'

'Tell me anyway. But let's start off with two of the more common solutions. First, a little bit of Vitamin D for mood elevation. Second, exercise. So let's walk.'

Suddenly, Kabuki was up off her seat and out the door.

Orla followed Kabuki up Hunter Street.

It was near empty – a few people wandered around, lost and hung-over. Orla noticed Kabuki had the same slight lag in the feet as Rhonda did, but that was the only sign she wasn't human.

'Are sudden walks part of the therapy?' Orla asked. 'It feels unusual.'

'I take a flexible approach,' said Kabuki. She took a deep breath through her nostrils and looked to the darkening sky. 'I smell a storm coming.'

'Are you sure you want to keep going?'

'No time like the present. I love the drama of a thunderstorm.'

'What if you get struck by lightning?'

'Zapped, schmapped.'

Orla was already panting on the uphill ascent. Kabuki was practically power walking.

'So,' said Kabuki, 'tell me how you're going to make yourself better.'

'Well,' said Orla. 'I've been reading a lot of self-help and all of it says I should socialise even when I don't feel like it.'

'Good start.'

'Also, my mind apparently shapes my own reality. So constant rumination isn't healthy.'

'Correct.'

'But don't you think it's weird, tricking myself that things are good when they aren't?'

'It's a matter of distorted perspective. The melancholic mind tends to remember the negative and discount the positive.'

'But what if I'm sad because I can see things clearly?'

'Some of the most intelligent people in the world experience negative events and yet choose happiness. But,' Kabuki continued, 'we're getting ahead of ourselves. I want you to start with the basics. Like, pick up a hobby.'

'A hobby?'

'Pick anything.'

'What would I do? Do you have a hobby?'

'I act in my spare time.'

'Really?'

'Yeah. I like the idea of total immersion. Understanding human motivation at its deepest levels. People even say I have the charisma of De Niro in his *Taxi Driver* years.'

'But De Niro's a guy.'

'I guess I have cross-over appeal.'

The sky cracked and rain gushed. It got into Orla's flats, and streamed down the gutters. The wind picked up and blew Orla's hair across her face.

Kabuki strode on unconcerned.

'Isn't it a treat to be alive!'

By the time they reached the Royal Botanic Garden, Orla was drenched through. Kabuki showed no signs of wanting to turn back.

They walked towards the harbour and ended up at the water, the Harbour Bridge visible in the distance.

On the grass to the right of a large tree, a few dozen white wooden chairs had been set up in two sections. An aisle of pink and white rose petals ran between them. Here and there, petals skipped in the wind. Women clutching white umbrellas kissed hello, holding their billowing silk dresses down at the sides. Two tourists in shorts stood by, cameras ready.

'A wedding!' said Kabuki. 'I love weddings.'

'Who gets married on New Year's Day?' Orla muttered.

'Let's be wedding guests.'

Kabuki grabbed Orla's hand. They sidled up to stand behind the white folding chairs, next to small children in clear rain ponchos hiding behind their fathers' legs. The children rubbed their eyes and howled at the wind.

'Don't you think it's a bit sociopathic?' said Orla. 'Joining a stranger's wedding?'

'We're not discussing me. You're the one in therapy.'

The wedding photographer raced up and stuck a lens in Orla's face.

'Twins?' she asked.

'She's my—'

'Sister,' said Kabuki, and hugged Orla's shoulder.

'Beautiful,' said the photographer, snapping away. 'Just beautiful. How do you know the bride?'

'We're colleagues, actually,' said Kabuki. 'She's stunning, isn't she? Just stunning.'

Orla watched the bridal party approach. The bride beamed, even though she was nearly lost in a dress made of infinite layers of fluff. Three bridesmaids in aqua followed. Each pulled along a gigantic round white balloon, tail adorned with coloured paper tassels. The balloons were acting up, trying to pull themselves free at every moment.

Everyone stood for the bride. A quartet began to play. But the music could barely be heard over a sudden gust of wind that blew the bride's dress up above her head and kept it there. She let out a bloodcurdling scream. She wasn't wearing underwear – just a triangular patch of blond hair.

The bridesmaids shrieked and let go of their balloons. They rushed to pull the dress down, battling the layers.

The dress stayed up for what seemed to Orla to be a glorious eternity. The photographer's camera fluttered. Guests sighed in sympathy. Parents clapped their hands over the eyes of their small children, who squealed in anger. The wedding celebrant, in a voice of rising panic, asked for calm.

Orla watched the balloons escape up and over the harbour, disappearing into the sky, tassels streaming. She looked from the vagina to the balloons and back to the vagina again.

She laughed and laughed and laughed.

They walked back to Wynyard.

'I was right, wasn't I?' said Kabuki. 'Crashing a wedding – fantastic.'

'Best start to the year ever. I feel bad about laughing.'

'You know, life's about meaningful experience,' said Kabuki. 'You need to be out in the world connecting with that. And you need to be eating right. Are you eating right? Lots of leafy greens?'

'Can't really afford them,' said Orla. 'But I'll try.'

Orla felt like things were looking up. She would go home and make a salad and get on the stationary bike and take up a hobby – maybe cross-stitch.

Behind the reception desk, Kabuki printed her off some material.

'These are worksheets on perfectionism,' said Kabuki. 'They'll help you improve your tolerance when the world falls short of your expectations, as well as your ability to accept the state of things when you can't change them.'

Orla looked at the worksheets.

'Are these spelling mistakes deliberate?'

Kabuki laughed. 'Time's up. Next week it's down to serious business. We'll discuss some medication options, and map your life across six domains to make sure you're on the optimal path for success.'

'Sounds good,' said Orla.

Kabuki shook her hand. 'I'll leave you with Rhonda to make our next appointment. One week from today should be fine.'

Orla was about to exit through the glass doors downstairs when she remembered the client drinks for *Rising Tide*. They clashed with the appointment she'd just made.

She took the lift back up to the office and found Rhonda slumped over her desk, unconscious.

'Oh my God. Rhonda?'

She shook Rhonda's shoulders but got no response. Rhonda's body felt rigid, like she was locked into place. Orla put two fingers on Rhonda's neck to check for a pulse, then remembered that Rhonda was a robot.

What am I doing? she thought.

She hurried down the corridor to the consultation room.

'Kabuki?' she said, knocking on the door. She turned

the handle. The door clicked open.

No one seemed to be in the office. There was an odd gap in the corner of the room. One of the walls seemed out of place, as if it had slid to one side. She could hear Kabuki's voice coming from behind it.

'Yeah, drinks would be great,' Kabuki was saying. 'Talking to losers all day is such a fucking drain. Just pack up the chairs, bring the dress back to the office. That sudden wind, though – perfect! Unrehearsable! Yeah, let's get wasted, forget work. Just give me some time to freshen up? Gotta get this fugly suit off and find a hotter one. Sure. Twenty minutes?'

Orla stepped through the opening.

She found herself in near darkness. Kabuki was facing away from her.

'Half an hour, then,' Kabuki said. 'Meet you out back.'

Kabuki pulled out what looked like an earpiece and dropped it on the carpet. Then, with one hand, she reached back to the nape of her neck, dug her nails into the flesh, and began to pull. Her neck and microchip and hair and scalp started to separate from the rest of her body. She kept pulling the flesh up and forward over her head. Her ears and face peeled off with the rest, in one continuous piece.

Underneath was a shining wet skull – a twisted network of metal balanced on metal vertebrae.

A strange fleshy odour, sweet and foul, filled Orla's nostrils. She gasped.

The android spun around, holding Orla's replica head by the hair. The android's own head had two eyeballs and a set of teeth fixed onto it.

'Orla?' said the metal face.

'Hi, I—'

'Isn't Rhonda out front?'

'She's—'

'Oh,' said the face. 'Recharging. Rhonda's so ancient she still has a bloody model number – Réception 3600.'

Orla watched the android toss the head onto a nearby chair, and then climb out of Orla's replica body.

'Sorry,' said the android, looking down at her metal skeleton. 'You got me at an awkward moment. What exactly did you overhear?'

It was then that Orla saw how far back the room extended. Along the three walls, queued up on hooks, were dozens of Kabuki's 'suits'. Each was suspended in a clear plastic pouch, like a giant IV bag, filled with dark yellow liquid. Orla squinted. One of the nearer ones looked a bit like Rabbit. It was hard to tell, without a skeleton filling it out.

The android seemed to lose interest in Orla, and turned to scan her collection.

'Who do I feel like putting on today?' she murmured.

She paced up and down the room until she decided on the suit she fancied. She entered a number into an interface next to Orla, and the hook bearing the chosen suit swung down the line towards them.

The android pulled out her eyeballs and teeth and flung them onto the carpet. The eyes bounced at Orla's feet.

She punctured the bag with her claws and ripped it apart. Liquid flowed out, soaking the floor. She felt around in the bag for her new set of eyeballs and teeth, and pushed them onto her face.

She took the selected scalp, stretched it over her skull like a swimming cap, and pulled the new face into position.

Suddenly, the android was blond, with full lips and blue eyes and a cute button nose.

She pulled the rest of the body from the bag, stepped into its toes and pulled it up over her frame. Her bones lengthened to fill the suit.

Her thighs and arms were thin, her stomach was flat. She adjusted her breasts. They bounced in just the right way.

She took a towel and dried off the liquid. She raised one arm and tilted her head upwards. Hot air blasted from somewhere above. As her hair dried, she closed her eyes and moved her head sensually from side to side. She tossed her lustrous locks. They cascaded in perfect waves.

Finally, she pulled a sky blue dress over her head and shoulders, and nearly lost her balance as she slid her feet into a pair of pink suede pumps.

'How do I look?' she said, in a new, husky voice. 'Everything in place?'

Orla nodded. The android looked and sounded exactly like the sniffling blond from the lift.

'You look shocked,' said the android. 'Come on, let's be real. It's hardly the singularity. What else can I do? Creep around town like a four-legged metallic praying mantis? This is a client who never has fun. I'm just taking her out for a spin in my spare time. Think of me as a voyeur into dysfunction – makes me a better therapist, don't you think?'

Kabuki turned to a mirror hanging on the back of the sliding wall. She pulled out a syringe and injected its contents into her lips. She lined her lips with pencil and shaded them in with hot-pink lipstick. She popped an index finger into her mouth and pulled it out.

'Don't want lipstick on our teeth, do we?' she said, admiring her inflated pout.

'No,' said Orla.

'Well, better be off. Got my cutest face on and no one to show it to. Best if you don't say a word to anyone. Parent Company's trade secrets, more or less. You understand. I'll see you next week.'

'I don't think so,' said Orla.

The android smoothed her hair in the mirror. Her gaze met Orla's and her new set of teeth glinted in the dark.

'Then, my darling,' she cooed, 'time is really up.'

The Fat Girl in History

My mother and I are sitting in front of the TV. We're talking about going on the CSIRO Total Wellbeing Diet.

I've filled in a preliminary form on the official Diet website. Based on my responses, it tells me that I'm Overweight, and that if I do the Diet, I could lose up to 8.3 kilograms in twelve weeks.

I feel relieved that I am Overweight and not Obese because there's less work to do and I'm lazy like that. This sort of thinking is more or less how I became Overweight in the first place.

'If you lose weight, Julie,' my mother says, 'when we walk down the street everyone will turn and say, "What a beautiful girl that lady is walking with!"'

'I'm already beautiful,' I tell my mother. 'All mothers should think their daughters are beautiful, all of the time.'

My mother is becoming upset about her sagging chin and arms, and her sagging everything in general. She's in her mid-sixties but looks like she's in her early fifties.

'You should be grateful,' I say. 'Other women your age

don't look as young as you do. Imagine if you actually looked your age. You would absolutely die.'

I remind her that I've never had skin as nice and clear and white as hers used to be when she was young. Everyone ages, I tell her. She should be glad she even got to be pretty in the first place. Some people go through their lives ugly, from start to finish.

She doesn't look convinced. She touches the slackening skin under her jawline, as if to see if it has miraculously tightened.

The problem everyone has with my body is not really that I am heavy-boned for a woman in general, but that I am heavy-boned for an Asian woman.

My university boyfriend, the one I thought I would marry, used to squeeze my arms and legs and call me Chunky Monkey. I was over 8.3 kilograms lighter in those days. He'd probably call me a Fail Whale now.

I once told him I wanted to buy a backless dress. It'd make me look chic, like I was from Paris or something.

'Don't you need a nice back to wear a backless dress?' he'd said.

In that moment, I suddenly became aware that not only did I have thunder thighs and a belly and adult acne and a fat head, but I also had a back that didn't look good from the back.

So I didn't buy a backless dress. I bought a hessian sack that covered my body from my neck to my knees, so that no one could tell if there was a woman underneath or a glutinous green blob with an unsightly green behind.

I'm sitting on a train wearing my hessian sack. I look at all the petite yellow women around me in a tableau determined by seating preferences and station order. Each little woman takes up just half of her blue seat. Overweight can look Obese when you're comparing yourself to delicate yellow peonies who blow gracefully in the wind.

I sit there and think about how they're all so tiny that I could squash them.

I also think about all the white guys I've met lately who have yellow fever. Even they reject me now. I'm not petite and Asian enough. I reject them and they reject me, and we are all filled with horrible feelings of rejection.

At a friend's wedding I'll be attending in the near future, I will avoid the dance floor and instead accost a friend's mother and complain to her about my dating woes – in particular, the phenomenon of yellow fever.

'Maybe,' she will say, 'the overwhelming attraction of some white men to exclusively Asian women is biologically the unconscious subjugation of one race by another.'

I like this theory. I like the idea that I am fighting a civilisational battle using my vagina.

I think that my heavy bones must be an indication that we have had a robust Russian somewhere in the family line, or maybe a Viking.

I order a DNA ancestry test kit online. When it comes in the mail, all I need to do is spit into a tube and post it back.

The lab sends the results by courier. I sign for the box. Inside the box is a pretty snow globe that fits in the palm of my hand. I stare into it.

In the background of the snow globe is the double helix logo of the DNA testing company. In the foreground is a tiny figurine of a big man in traditional Cossack gear. He's standing in the snow shielding a little Chinese woman from the weather by wrapping her in the folds of the coat he's wearing. Her shoes are at least six sizes too small. In fluent Mandarin, he's telling her that she will bear him gigantic, beautiful semi-Slav babies. She smiles and blinks. Snowflakes cling to her eyelashes.

'Of course,' I say out loud. 'My blood's part-Russian, not Viking.'

This should already have been clear to me, given that I've never had any upper body strength. I'm unable to lift a finger, let alone row a boat from Scandinavia to China.

'Can a lab be this specific about my ethnicity?' I ask myself. I revisit the website of the DNA testing company. I realise that the company specialises not only in DNA Testing but also in DNA Wish Fulfilment, and that I've unwittingly ticked the optional Wish Fulfilment box at the end of my test kit request.

I don't care. Because the lab has confirmed my wish that we've had a Russian in the family, I start to drink vodka. I try all the brands.

I am connecting with my roots.

Despite plying myself with alcohol, I have niggling doubts. If the reason for my fatness cannot squarely be laid at the feet of a giant Russian, then I have to conclude that it's probably my own fault.

One evening when I'm not drunk, I go to Fitness Second for an introductory session with a personal trainer.

I distract him from training me by asking him in-depth questions about his personal life. He's happy to talk. He has a girlfriend who was once a client. His father is Greek, and keeps tarantulas.

Despite my conversational manoeuvres, my personal trainer still manages to prepare worksheets for me that set out the different exercises I need to do every day.

When I come back to the gym the next evening, he takes me through the circuit he has designed for me, so that my technique is correct.

We do a lot of work with exercise balls. We also box. I put gloves on and punch the pads he's holding up. After five minutes, I get tired and bored.

'I'm puffed,' I say.

We go to Gloria Jean's instead for iced coffees topped with cream.

This is how I gain fat by going to the gym.

While I'm shedding kilos unsuccessfully, everything turns out well for my mother.

The front door is open when I arrive home after my iced coffee. The porch light is off; the house is dark.

'Is that you, Julie?' my mother calls out.

'What's wrong?'

'Come into the lounge room.'

The lounge room is set up like a photography studio, with a cyclorama where our altar for the Goddess of Mercy used to be. In the near darkness, a woman is standing side on, turning her face to smile enigmatically at a clicking camera.

'Work it, work it, work it,' the photographer is saying.

The woman is slim and beautiful, with fine alabaster skin. She's wearing a black backless gown. A diamond-encrusted pendant on a long silver chain hangs down her back.

'It happened,' she says to me in my mother's voice. 'It's a miracle! I'm young again! And I'm the new face of Chanel.'

My friend Jiao comes back from Hollywood to get rid of the last of his Sydney belongings.

We go to Obelisk Beach on New Year's Day. We aren't really beach people, but lately I've given up hope that one day I'll live in a place that snows at the turn of each year. By going to the beach, I feel that I am embracing my Australianness. I've picked Obelisk Beach because I want to avoid the crowds. Obelisk is apparently one of the most secluded beaches in Sydney. It's also a nudist beach for gay men.

On the way there, I ask Jiao what the rules are at a gay nudist beach. Is it okay to be a woman? Is it rude to wear my swimming costume?

Jiao says it's fine for us both to keep our clothes on.

To access the beach from the road, we have to climb down a huge rock staircase. There are a lot of bushes around. I've read on the internet that men 'cruise' here. As we move down the stairs, I wonder why anyone would want to have sex among rocks and bushes. These are gay men, after all. Don't they want fluffy pillows and thousand-thread-count

Egyptian cotton sheets? Who will maintain the world's standards for classy living, if not gay men?

The beach is small and quite crowded. Not all the beach-goers are men, but most are. Three-quarters of the people here are nude.

It's definitely rude to look at all the penises, but I sneak glances anyway. They look so small, and this surprises me because so many of their kind have gone to war and conquered cities and engineered financial collapses and been models for very tall buildings.

Jiao and I lay out our towels, sit down and talk.

'Should we go into the water?' Jiao asks after a while.

'Sure,' I say, nonchalant. I start undressing, down to my swimming costume.

I'm really worried about my big thighs and belly. I try to keep them covered for as long as possible, then I get up and wobble with them across the few metres of sand between our towels and the water. I wade in as quickly as possible.

Two boats are moored just off the beach. One is full of people: men in shorts and a woman in a black dress. They're flying a rainbow flag and playing old-time jazz.

I'm very comfortable here. No one's ogling me, and no one seems bothered that I'm the wrong gender and sexual orientation. No one here is even really swimming. Like Jiao and me, most people are just standing around in the water or floating on their backs. The sand is smooth, except for some occasional rocks. There aren't any violent waves, so I don't feel like I'm going to be pulled under suddenly and delivered to the Kraken. The water just laps in and out.

I'm still curious about the penises of everyone on the beach. The more I consider them, the more it becomes apparent that the penises only tend to look small because a lot of men here have big bellies, which dwarf their other body parts.

I compare the size of each paunch to its corresponding penis. I decide to call it the Paunch to Penis Ratio.

A man with what I am sure is a very high Paunch to Penis Ratio wades over and begins to talk to me. It's not clear to me if he's gay or not. I get more of a paedophilic vibe from him. I remain calm, reminding myself that although I'm emotionally still a child, I am currently the size of an adult.

The man tells me a bit about the history of the area but I don't retain any of it. Something about there being a golf course here in years gone by.

'You look a bit out of place here,' he says.

'Why's that?'

'You look very white.'

'I've been sitting indoors writing,' I say. 'I haven't seen any sun.'

'I guess you and your boyfriend are here having a cultural experience?' he says.

I look back at the beach, at all the other beachgoers. I realise that, in their eyes, Jiao and I must look like we're tourists from China who got waylaid on our way to Bondi and are unsure what to do about it.

'It's a *gay* beach,' says the Paunch. He says the *gay* under his breath as if it's a secret.

'Yeah, I know,' I say. 'I guess I qualify because I brought my gay friend?'

'It's nice you're here,' says the Paunch. 'It's nice to have some eye candy once in a while.'

The water is at chest level for both of us. I realise that, underneath, the Paunch's junk is just floating there, cradled by salt water. I'm not only meeting the Paunch for the first time, I am also meeting his junk.

The Paunch is now standing between Jiao and me, and gradually edging forward. He asks me what country I'm from, and talks about how he spends six months of the year in Thailand.

Jiao keeps looking over, then leaves the water to go lie on the beach.

'What do you write?' the Paunch asks.

I tell him I write fiction but am having a crisis of confidence. A review of my work has just been published in *The Australian Morning Age*.

'The reviewer said my fiction is bland,' I tell him. 'I think it's a typo. I think he meant to type "wild".'

I tell the Paunch that I wonder if my yellow skin and vagina are limiting my chances at being the next big Australian author. I tell him that I stand in the shower sometimes and try to scrub the yellow off but, huh, it turns out it doesn't work like fake tan. I ask him if I can borrow his body and perhaps his mind.

'Ha ha,' he says nervously, paddling backwards.

Judy Garland appears on the deck of the boat that is flying the rainbow flag. She gazes down at me. She's in her younger years and is holding a small dog and looking wistful, as if she is feeling very stuck and can't leave.

'I tell you who's funny, Judy,' I say to her from the water, 'your daughter Liza. Is really very funny.'

Judy begins to sing. She sings about a rainbow somewhere. She sings away all the layers of anxiety I didn't even know I had.

I tell her I'm a writer.

'What have you written recently?' she says.

I tell her I've just finished a short story about a young woman who has depression. I finished it on New Year's Eve and went to sleep at nine o'clock, like the woman in the story.

'How much of the story is true?' Judy asks.

'Well, it's about androids in the future, so …'

'Uh huh,' says Judy. 'Okay.'

She feeds her little dog a biscuit treat.

'Is your work popular?' she asks.

'I don't think so. I think I'm behind the times. Everyone's writing about celebrities now. Like, inserting famous people into their fiction.'

'Interesting device,' says Judy. 'A bit gimmicky.'

Back on the beach, Jiao is burning. The skin on his back is all red.

We agree that it's time to go, and begin to climb back up the rock staircase.

'That guy in the water,' I say. 'I think he was coming on to me. I also felt like he might be a paedophile.'

'Oh,' says Jiao, 'I thought he was just making conversation. He seemed like a nice guy.'

I am dying, climbing up these stairs. At the top, I try to control my panting so it seems that I'm breathing regularly, like a fit person. I almost keel over.

On the way back to the car, Jiao gives me life advice.

'If I were you, I'd write genre fiction to fund your literary fiction. Vampires or something. And get back on OkCupid. You can't find a partner if you're locked away writing every day. How is anyone going to marry you if they don't know you exist? I don't want to come back and see you when you're forty years old, bitter because all the good guys are married off and you've missed out on finding the right one for you.'

'I hate OkCupid. It's so unromantic.'

'Oh, no,' he says. 'You're not still in love with the Kerouac guy, are you?'

I've had a multi-year crush on a dark-haired guy who's a fan of Jack Kerouac.

He's three years younger than me. I barely know him. Nevertheless, I've tried to woo him with clever variations on the metaphysical love poetry of Andrew Marvell. Unfortunately, the romantic success I pictured when writing those poetic variations far exceeded their real-world reception.

I ask my crush what he likes to read.

'I like *On the Road*,' he says. 'I like that the style was based on jazz.'

I neglect to tell him that I didn't enjoy *On the Road*, and that I like actual jazz – not jazz fiction.

My crush mostly ignores me, most of the time. I wonder

if he'll start liking me if I become more like Jack Kerouac. I send him love letters filled with sharp fives and flat nines.

All he says is, 'Thanks.'

Eventually, I realise that he won't start liking me if I become more like Jack. *He* wants to be Jack. He doesn't want *me* to be Jack.

In a surprising and upsetting turn of events, he ends up falling madly in love with my mother, the Chanel model.

He can't stop texting her. He develops RSI in his thumbs from texting her so much. He texts her even while I'm talking to him about the beauty of *On the Road*, and how my fiction could one day be as cool and famous as Jack's.

In practically no time, my mother asks him to move in with her. This means that I have to move out.

'Aren't you troubled by the age difference?' I ask her.

'You're thirty-two,' says my mother. 'You've always had a hard time dealing with reality. Wallowing in dreams is not going to improve your circumstances. It's time for you to wake up and learn to support yourself financially. I am having my second wind. Go and have your first.'

My mother and my crush, a glamorous item, have a big booze-up at their place to celebrate Australia Day. All their smug couple friends are there.

They party all night, but they push everyone out by sunrise. It turns out that, despite my crush's baby-face, he's a four-hundred-year-old vampire. The age difference between him and my mother is no longer an issue.

On my way out the front door, he shakes a long, bony finger at me.

'If you dare write about me in your genre fiction,'

he says, 'I will suck you dry and chuck your body in a Woolworths dumpster.'

I tell Jack Kerouac about my woes when he turns up in the front yard of the apartment block where I'm living.

He has reincarnated, and is currently a forty-five-year-old who owns a one-person company that mows lawns in our neighbourhood.

The landlord hates listening to Jack blather on, so I've volunteered to go out into the yard on a fortnightly basis to give Jack the envelope with his thirty-dollar mowing fee.

The beauty of Jack is that he knows all the gossip about all the people on the street. He just offers it without me asking as I'm giving him the cash – as if it's part of the trade. He tells me who's moving in and out, how much all the apartments have sold for, who is having an affair with whom, and who has gone on holiday and killed themselves.

I tell Jack about my struggles as a writer. I remind him of the paper scroll he typed on to produce *On the Road*, and how the scroll sold at auction for more than two million dollars.

'That's about right,' he says. 'But that was literally a lifetime ago. Get with the program.'

Jack isn't interested in Genius or Literature anymore, only Gossip.

I complain to Jack about being a woman and a writer.

I tell him that men are brought up to be bold. That they become the sorts of people who'll put on a pair of boxing gloves, dip the gloves in paint, and then punch art across a canvas. They blaze through and fall down and pick themselves up.

I tell him that women are born bold but then people chip away at them. "'Don't do this, don't do that," everyone says, "or you'll make mistakes. And if you ever get important enough to sit on a stage in front of an audience, for God's sake, close your legs.'"

'Stop bitching,' says Jack. 'Start producing.'

I suddenly decide that Jack is handsome, and ask if he'd like to go out on a date.

'I'm in love with Joan slash Laura,' he says.

'Who?'

'You didn't read my book properly, did you? Should've known. Even the way you make me talk isn't natural. If you think *On the Road*'s a mess, this story's even worse. Where's the cohesive narrative? Where's the structure? It's just a bunch of anecdotes about being fat. It's a fucking mélange.'

'Like a mélange à trois?'

'What are you even saying?'

I think Jack is being unfair. I don't know much about him but I know a lot about other writers. Salinger, for instance. I watched a documentary about Salinger once. If Jack were Salinger, this conversation would have been a lot more historically and linguistically accurate.

'Well, this is my advice,' says Jack. 'If you want to succeed, you first have to identify which writers you are having a dialogue with in this country.'

'I'm not sure I'm having a dialogue with anyone.'

'You think you're hollering into the darkness but you're

not. You're having a conversation with someone but you just don't know who it is yet.'

'Maybe it's Peter Carey,' I say. 'People say I remind them of Peter Carey.'

'He must be after my time.'

'I haven't read any Peter Carey.'

Jack walks back to his lawnmower and starts it up. 'If you sound like Peter Carey but you haven't read any Peter Carey,' he shouts over the roar of the machine, 'maybe you're reinventing a perfectly good wheel.'

I stand there thinking about what he's said. I decide that the writer I must be having a dialogue with is actually a guy called Tom, basically because I stalk him and we literally exchange words as a result. I also talk to another writer called Eric, who sends me creepy stories about terrariums, and tells me that if I want to be a proper writer, all I need to do is stand on a desk and declare that I am one.

I conclude that making note of actual conversations I've had is probably the best way to keep tabs on who I'm talking to.

Over breakfast, I'm reading an article about current trends in fiction. The author contends that society is now in the throes of autofiction. Everyone is writing it; everyone is reading it. Everyone wants to read about *real* alcoholic fathers, and *real* divorces, and *real* stay-at-home dads. No one wants anyone to make shit up anymore.

The author also claims that the days of postmodernism and pastiche are over.

I don't even know what pastiche is. It sounds like a type of pastie filled with Clag.

I skim the rest of the article and finish my porridge. I decide that I'm going to write an autofictional essay called 'The Fat Girl in History'.

I'm following the hip literary crowd. I'm deliberately in vogue.

I'm selling myself out but at least I'm selling myself to you.

I'm invited to the wedding of one of my best friends.

Everyone is shaking hands in the foyer, waiting to proceed into the ballroom. The women around me are wearing stacks of bangles and beautiful make-up. I can't understand a word they're saying. I used to go to school with them. We used to speak the same language.

'Umf umf umf,' they say, kissing me on both cheeks. The bangles rattle around me.

'Fug fug fug,' one of their husbands says, putting an arm around my shoulder.

'Ik ik?' I ask, trying to blend in. I don't know what I'm trying to say.

They look at me like I'm not making any sense.

I try a different tack.

'Audi?' I say. 'Lexus gucci prada tiffany?'

They smile and nod, and I smile and nod.

I look at them and my brain is a blank field below a blank sky. No thoughts appear; no ideas for conversation occur to me.

They proffer a camera, and I take a photo of them and

their husbands and babies. Their arms are very toned, and their teeth are very white.

The bride puts her arm through mine and leads me to the bathroom. We stand at the mirrors as she fixes her hair.

'Am I losing my mind?' I ask. 'Do you understand what I'm saying?'

'Og og *quog* og,' she says, adjusting her sari and refreshing her lipstick.

'Shit,' I say. 'My life is over.'

She smiles at me in the mirror. 'Kidding.'

I smile back. She has the most beautiful face in the world.

'But,' she adds, 'you should stop telling people about Jack and Judy.'

'What?'

'At least Jiao's real, right?'

'You're all real.'

In bed, I watch a documentary on my laptop about women who are extremely fat, and deliberately continue to make themselves bigger. Many have skinny romantic partners who become their 'feeders'. The feeders enjoy feeding their women to fatten them up.

Men make appointments to spend time with these women, just so the women will sit on them.

It's a smart idea. There are a few people out there whom I'd be happy to crush, especially if they paid for it.

When the documentary is over, I lie down and look into the very core of my nature. I discover that I am simultaneously extremely ambitious and extremely lazy. It becomes apparent to me that an ambition appropriate to this core nature is to be the fattest person that ever lived, and to achieve this by being too lazy to exercise.

So I eat. I fatten myself up like a Wagyu cow.

Each roll of fat gets bigger and bigger until it rolls over the previous roll, grows downwards, and puts down roots.

My rolls spread out over the front yard and the whole apartment block.

I work harder at eating and soon the rolls extend across the country. Kangaroos hop across my knees. Black cockatoos make their nests in the crooks of my elbows. Koalas climb up and hug themselves around my pinkie fingers.

I can see how big I'm getting relative to the people who come around to visit. They lift up my arm fat and pop under it and say hello.

They're all so small that I have to squint to see them. Although they start out chatting to me in an upbeat mood, every one of them ends up lamenting my weight. It's like someone's died. Their tears form puddles around my ankles. Platypuses paddle in the salt water.

I continue to expand in ever-multiplying concentric rings of fat, which move outwards across the world. Soon there is no more room for oceans, let alone tears. I am one big beach.

I begin to grow extra limbs and heads and breasts. Nevertheless, my Paunch to Penis Ratio remains nil.

I have so many fingers and arms and legs and necks now, that I am able to wear truckloads of statement jewellery. I adorn myself with malachite and onyx, moss agate and lapis lazuli, citrine and smoky quartz. My jewellery becomes beautiful armour.

I become the face of Fat Chanel, and they send a team of photographers to shoot me from every angle. They do so even though they're in the middle of a stressful trade mark dispute over the unauthorised use of the Chanel name.

I wear a backless dress for the key promo shot. The dress is also frontless, shoulderless and arseless.

They build a white temple to contain me. The walls are made of square panels that interlock in an ingenious way, so that new sections of wall can be added easily as I expand.

I grow faster than the little people can build the walls.

Around the temple, under an orange sky, a field of yellow peonies springs up.

Millions of ant-sized people pick the peonies and bring them to me as offerings. They lay them at my feet. They are here to get my blessing – for their newborns and marriages and assorted happy occasions – because I have become a goddess who doesn't care about shit, and people really respond to that.

I gather up all the tiny worshippers and their fragile peonies. I pick up all the people I love and the people I hate – Jack and Judy, and Jiao and the Paunch, and Tom and Eric, and my mother and her vampire, and my friend with the beautiful face, and all the little women with their rattling bangles and words I don't understand.

I wrap my fat arms around all of these little people, and hug them to my breast. I drug them with a lullaby, and nurse them all to sleep.

Snow begins to fall.

In their dreams, the little people call out to me. They call me the Goddess of Mercy.

Because I can nurse them or I can crush them, and the power is all mine.

Acknowledgements

Thanks to my parents and sister, unwavering sources of love and support.

Particular thanks to my kind and incredibly gifted editor, Ian See, who made this book happen. 'Sight' is dedicated to him.

Thanks to Madonna Duffy, Rachel Crawford, Lucille Cruise-Burns and everyone at UQP, for bringing me in from the wilderness. To Josh Durham, for his crazy cool cover design. To Amanda Lohrey, for her generosity and guidance.

Thanks to the first editors and publishers of stories in this collection, especially Louise Swinn and Zoe Dattner of Sleepers Publishing, who put me on the literary map in Australia. Thanks also to Sam Cooney and Johannes Jakob at *The Lifted Brow*; Kalinda Ashton; Suzanne Kamata at *Kyoto Journal*; Emily Stewart, Alice Grundy and David M Henley at *Seizure*; *The Best Australian Stories* team at Black Inc.; and Khairani Barokka, Ng Yi-Sheng, Amir Muhammad and the Fixi Novo team. A wink and salute to Matt Huynh and Gee Hale, who illustrated a number of these stories when they were first published.

If you hate my wild slash bland writing, attribute partial blame to schoolteachers of mine who nurtured it in its infancy – including Greig "Grobbo" Robinson, Annette Wright, Diane Alchin, Matthew Wood, Eleni Tatsis, Jan Roberts and Barbara Stone. Lay some additional blame on my writing teacher, Dr Stephen Carver, to whom 'Inquiry Regarding the Recent Goings-On in the Woods' is dedicated.

My gratitude extends to the following people for their encouragement and support during the transition from law to fiction, and in relation to this book: Jiao Chen, Tara Sarathy, Alexandra Marie Brown, Michael Camilleri, Gary Lo, Brett Millar, Eric Yoshiaki Dando, Andrew McGovern, Jane Chi Hyun Park, HK Tang, Anna Zhu, Alison Cole, Dave Smith, Philip Amos, Grant Scicluna, Bethany Bruce, Donna Chang, Xin Li, Stephanie Han, Tom Cho, Tash Aw, Haline Ly, Jacqui Dent, Vasudha Srinivasan, Suchitra Krishnan, Clem Cairns, Dr Kevin Walton, Geoff Orton, Laurie Steed, Luke Thomas, Daniel Young, John Fenech, Elisabeth Kramer, Tiffany Tsao, Kenny Leck, Renée Ting, Jon Gresham, Karma Chahine, Nicola O'Shea, Natalie Kestecher, Alex Adsett, Bridget Lutherborrow, Tara Cartland, Darby Hudson, Pierz Newton-John, the Betts family, John Bell and Ben Wood, Jack and Judy. I'd also like to thank Andrew and Patricia Su, Hagen Bluhm, Chua Boon Ching, Angie Lee and my extended family, as well as Todd Hodgson, Eronnie Samuels, Oskar Henning, Andrew Nott, Mouse Maroney and the gang at Soundworks Studios.

Many more people have crossed my path than are listed here. Thanks to those who've believed in my writing, and have done their best to help me on my way.

Publication details

'Sight', *Kyoto Journal*, Issue 80, 2014.

'Civility Place', *The Sleepers Almanac No. 9*, eds Louise Swinn and Zoe Dattner, Sleepers Publishing, 2014; and *The Best Australian Stories 2014*, ed. Amanda Lohrey, Black Inc., 2014.

'The Three-Dimensional Yellow Man', *The Lifted Brow Digital Edition*, Volume 5 Issue 1, 2014.

'Two', *The Sleepers Almanac No. 8*, eds Zoe Dattner and Louise Swinn, Sleepers Publishing, 2013.

'The Procession', *HEAT*, eds Khairani Barokka and Ng Yi-Sheng, Fixi Novo, 2016.

'The Sister Company', *Seizure Online: Editions*, Edition 1, 2015.

'The Fat Girl in History', *The Sleepers Almanac X*, eds Zoe Dattner and Louise Swinn, Sleepers Publishing, 2015.

Also in UQP's short fiction series

PERIPHERAL VISION
Paddy O'Reilly

**'This is a great collection, which also burns
an impression on our imagination.'
Debra Adelaide, *Australian Book Review***

In her second collection of short stories, Paddy O'Reilly takes
us into the fringes of human nature – our hidden thoughts,
our darker impulses and our unspoken tragedies. By turns
elegiac and acerbic, but always acutely observed, *Peripheral
Vision* confirms O'Reilly as one of our most inventive and
insightful writers.

'A writer of considerable poise and ingenuity …
O'Reilly's imagination is never predictable, and her
readers will thrill to the kinds of strange harmonies she
composes.' *Age/Sydney Morning Herald*

'Stellar … worth it for the staggeringly good "Procession"
alone.' Charlotte Wood, *Weekend Australian*, Best Books
of 2015

ISBN 978 0 7022 5360 7